Francis Plowden

# Impartial thoughts upon the beneficial consequences of inrolling all deeds, wills, and codicils affecting lands, throughout England and Wales

Francis Plowden

**Impartial thoughts upon the beneficial consequences of inrolling all deeds, wills, and codicils affecting lands, throughout England and Wales**

ISBN/EAN: 9783337207885

Printed in Europe, USA, Canada, Australia, Japan

Cover: Foto ©Andreas Hilbeck / pixelio.de

More available books at **www.hansebooks.com**

UPON THE

BENEFICIAL CONSEQUENCES

OF

# INROLLING

ALL

Deeds, Wills, and Codicils affecting Lands,

THROUGHOUT ENGLAND AND WALES.

BY

FRANCIS PLOWDEN, Esq.

CONVEYANCER.

LONDON:

PRINTED FOR E. BROOKE, IN BELL-YARD, TEMPLE-BAR.

M.DCC.LXXXIX.

## To the PUBLIC.

FROM my experience of the mifchiefs arifing from the imperfection of the prefent regiftering Acts for the Counties of York and Middlefex, as well as from the want of an univerfal Inrolment of Deeds and Wills affecting Land, I feel it my duty to apprize the public of the evil they are fuffering, and to fuggeft a remedy, that will not only eradicate the diforder, but add ftrength and vigour to the part affected. For the fatisfaction, however, of the public and of myfelf, I firft fubmitted it to the confideration of all the Judges and Law Officers of the country, to which I wifh it to be applied; moft of whom have done me the honour to exprefs the ftrongeft approbation of the plan, and a wifh to fee it carried into execution. I do not fay this with a view to bias the opinion of any individual, but to prove that I have acquitted myfelf of every preliminary duty to the public, before I prefented to them this publication.

It is now offered to them as the only mean, by which their previous fenfe of the expedient can be tried and known.

As it is my defign to reduce the feveral acts of parliament upon the fubject, to one plain, confiftent and efficient ftatute, I expect that a candid public will approve of my going rather largely into the inconfiftencies and mifchiefs of fuch acts, as I have thought neceffary to be repealed.

The

The confiderations, motives, and reafons for my digefting and propofing to the public a plan for an univerfal Inrolment of all Deeds and Wills affecting Land, will, I hope, have their full weight in forming the opinions of individuals upon the expediency of it. Thefe are, to the *Land Owner*, the encreafe of the value of his land, by clearing and confirming his title to it, and facilitating the means of fettling, charging, or felling it: to the *Monied Man*, the multiplication, certainty, and faith of land fecurities: to the *Lawyer*, the eafe, fatisfaction, and furety both of his client and himfelf in all negotiations refpecting lands: to the *Financier*, the general rife of the value of land in the market, which muft proportionably raife the price of the funds: and to the *Senator*, the good and quiet of the fubject, the confiftency and certainty of the law, and the welfare and profperity of the nation.

FRANCIS PLOWDEN.

*Adelphi Terrace.*

# CONTENTS.

*INTRODUCTION*, Page 1
*Reasons for the Publication*, 2
*Apology to the Profession*, 3
*General Ideas of our Law*, 3
*The ancient Tenures of Land in England*, 5
*The free Power of aliening Land in a commercial Country*, 6
*The Notoriety of the first Acts of Alienation of Land*, 7
*The Plausibility of popular Prejudices*, 11
*Proofs of the ancient Notoriety in the Alienation of Lands*, 14
*Of Uses*, 15
*Reasons of some Deeds not being inrolled*, 16
*Of Lands being deviseable*, 19
*Of the Introduction of Secret Conveyances*, 21
*Further Proofs of the ancient Notoriety of all Deeds affecting Lands*, 22
*The superior Necessity of such Notoriety in the present, more than in any past Age*, 24
*How Grievances are sometimes redressed in Parliament*, 27

*The*

*The Absurdity and Inefficacy of the 4th and 5th William and Mary, to prevent Fraud by clandestine Mortgages,* Page 31
*Of Notice,* 35
*The different Opinions of our Courts upon the Effects of Notice,* 39
*The Determination of all the Parliaments of France upon the Notice of a Deed registered,* 42
*Practical Applications to the foregoing Subjects,* 43
*The Cases of Rickman v. Morgan, and Pearson v. Morgan,* 46
*Of Title-Deeds,* 51
*A supposed Case upon a Title under Deeds not inrolled,* 52
*A real Case anonymous, upon fraudulent Mortgages,* 53
*Of the Registry of Deeds and Wills by different Acts of Parliament,* 53
*Of the Effects of certain Words in Deeds, and the modern Forms of Conveyances,* 67
*The Consequences of a Deed not registered,* 69
*The Consequences of a Deed registered,* 70
*The Mischiefs of the registering Acts,* 73
*A Registry ought to be a Conservatory of Men's Title-Deeds,* 75
*There appear to have been such Conservatories by the 5th Hen. IV. and by the 3d and 4th Edw. VI.* 76
*Of the Inrolment of Deeds by common Law,* 77
*Of the Acknowledgment of Deeds by common Law,* 80

Of

*Of the Involment of Deeds by Statute,* Page 82
*Of the Effects of inrolling Deeds,* 82
*Of the Inrolment of Roman Catholic's Deeds,* 86
*Of the Inconsistency of the* 11*th and* 12*th of Wil. III. and the* 3*d Geo. I.* 89
*Of the Inconveniences of the* 3*d Geo. I.* 91
*Of the unconstitutional Hardship of the* 3*d Geo. I.* 92
*Of further Inconveniences of the* 3*d Geo. I.* 93
*A supposed Case upon the Title of a Papist before the Repeal of any Part of the* 11*th and* 12*th of Wil. III.* 94
*Of the unintended Effects of repealing a Part of the* 11*th and* 12*th of Wil. III.* 95
*Experimental Effects of the* 3*d Geo. I.* 96
*Of the Decisions of our Courts upon the* 11*th and* 12*th of Wil. III.* 98
*Of the Inrolment of Deeds by a Judge's* Fiat, 105
*Of the Inrolment of Wills,* 110
*How the Right of Administration probably came to the Ordinary,* 114
*The Spiritual Courts had not the original Cognizance of Wills,* 116
*Lands were formerly deviseable,* 120
*The Norman Feudal System incompatible with the Power of devising Lands,* 121
*Of the different Modes of inrolling Deeds in the different Courts,* 123
*The Objections against the Notoriety of Deeds and Wills affecting Lands,* 127

Of

*Of the Absurdity of entering Devises of Land in a Court which has no Cognizance of them,* Page 129
*Draught of a Bill for requiring the Inrolment of all Deeds, &c. &c.* 134
*Observations upon the Draught of the Bill,* 179

IMPAR-

# IMPARTIAL THOUGHTS, &c.

## *Introductory Considerations.*

MOST persons are in the habit of allowing merit, and even of giving praise to every act, which proceeds from the legislative wisdom of the British parliament. Yet if we reflect coolly and deliberately upon the circumstances, under which acts of parliament are often passed, we shall find, from the motives, reasons, and occasions of bringing in the bill, the persons or party, by whom the business is managed and conducted, and the means, by which it is carried through the houses, that the real good of the country was not the principle, upon which the bill was grounded, and consequently, that the welfare of the country is not the consequence of its having passed into a law. It will be needless to adduce instances of this truth; since every person, who will bestow even a passing thought upon the subject, must call to his recollection many occurrences, to which it most forcibly applies. The personal wish of the Sovereign, the private views of a minister, the interest of a party, the concealed arts of interested individuals, the inconsiderable impetuosity of the proposers, the ignorance of the managers, the inexperience of the draftsmen, and the inattention of the members to what may not personally interest them, are the various

various causes of acts of parliament being amended, explained and repealed.

It is in fact impossible, that any human intuition can be so perfectly comprehensive, as to foresee and prevent many consequences of a law, which it was the intention and expectation of the legislators to have obviated in passing it. To some speculative minds, this may be a humiliating consideration; but it must convince every one, that upon any attempt to alter the law, it becomes highly adviseable to take every previous step to consult with and inform those persons in particular of the subject, who are competent to judge of, or who may be interested in or affected by the alteration. When this necessary precaution has been attended to, and the plan has been previously approved of, no responsibility can lie with those, under whose immediate sanction the proposal is brought forward and carried into execution.

*Reasons for this Publication.*

In the course of practice as a conveyancer, I have met with several instances, in which great advantages have been produced from a *regular inrolment* of deeds and wills affecting lands; and in which, very great inconveniences and important losses have been incurred and suffered from the *registry* of deeds and wills in certain counties, according to several acts of parliament now in force. Upon turning the subject repeatedly in my mind, I became decisively convinced of the expediency, and even necessity, of inrolling all deeds and wills affecting lands throughout England and Wales. With a view fairly to commit this expediency and necessity to the judgment of the public, I have ventured to commit my thoughts upon it to the press.

To provoke investigation and enquiry, is a demonstration of the intention to lead to truth.

*Apology.*

To the gentlemen of my profession, I must apologize for deviating in the course of my reasoning from that technical formality and precision, with which legal subjects are usually treated. My wish is to adapt my reasoning to non-professional minds, and make them as much masters of the subject, upon which they are now called upon to judge, as if they had devoted much of their time to the study of the law. I have also for these reasons been so particular and full in my quotations, as generally to save my readers the trouble of resorting to the books, from which I have taken them.

*General Ideas of our Law.*

*Semper eadem* is the respectable and wise device of our jurisprudence, which, as Lord Bacon says (*a*), *ever favours the law of nature*; and that stands upon no other basis. But it is not from the temporary variations and superficial appearances, that we are to judge of this sameness; it is the fundamental principle, to which we are to look up In the succession of ages, the variation of manners and customs, the diversity of languages, the variety of characters, in the monarchy of Solomon, the republic of Rome, and the government of Great Britain, from Lapland to the Brasils, one *same* principle of nature actuates the whole. So from the code of Alfred, to the present complicated mass of statutes and precedents in law and equity, through all the various forms and changes of our govern-

(*a*) Bacon's argument in the Exchequer Chamber on Calvin's case.

ment, the ſame principles, upon which the law was founded in its primitive ſimplicity, will be found to ſupport and uphold it in all its extent of multifarious modifications; as the ſame ſource of juices cauſes the acorn to ſplit, and feeds the luxuriant oak. I do not term that an innovation of the law, which is interwoven with its firſt principles: it often becomes requiſite, that particular laws ſhould be newly modelled and adapted to the exigencies of the preſent manners, times, and circumſtances. Upon this principle was it, that Mr. Locke, (*a*) in the 79th article of his Carolina laws, enacted, "that to avoid a multiplicity of laws, which by "degrees always change the right foundations of "the original government, all acts of parliament "whatſoever ſhall at the end of one hundred "years after their enacting, reſpectively ceaſe and "determine of themſelves without any repeal." For as, during the courſe of a century, many changes will neceſſarily take place in the cuſtoms, manners, and habits of the nation; ſo ſhould the laws alſo change with them: but as the former changes cannot be produced, but upon one invariable principle of nature, ſo ought not the latter to be varied nor newly modelled, but upon the original principles of the law.

The law of nature is the general ground-work of every municipal law; and the exigencies of civil ſociety have founded ſome general principles common to all communities: yet, from the locality, temperature, and other peculiarities of certain ſocieties, theſe principles have branched out into a great diverſity of laws. I ſhall paſs over the original rights acquired by occupancy, or claims eſtabliſhed in the law of nature; and take up our conſiderations from the cultivated ſtate of ſociety, when

(*a*) Locke's Works, Vol. III. p. 674.

this

this iſland, or at leaſt the ſouthern part of it, was eſtabliſhed in a regular and certain order of government.

*Reaſons of Policy.*

The geographical ſituation of this iſland, has adapted it peculiarly to all the purpoſes of trade and commerce: and it is eſſentially important to the welfare and flouriſhing ſtate of trade and commerce, that the landed property of the country ſhould be eſtabliſhed and kept upon ſuch a footing, as to render it ſerviceable and uſeful for all mercantile purpoſes. Thus land, to become uſeful to commerce, muſt be marketable and negociable; and to be ſo, muſt be invariably clear and evident in its title.

*Of the ancient Tenures of Land.*

The preſent modern tenures of lands in England and Wales, have inſenſibly formed themſelves into ſome reaſonable and conſiſtent principle, upon the gradual decline, and at length the total abolition of the feudal ſyſtem. It is curious to obſerve, that every affection of the land, even under the preſent tenures, is only accountable for upon ſome feudal principle. To anſwer my intended purpoſe, we will throw back our ideas to the year 800, at which time, Sir Henry Spelman ſays, the feudal ſyſtem was the law of nations in our weſtern world; for although in the time of our Saxon anceſtors, the feudal law had footing in this iſland, as well as in other parts of Europe, yet it was not attended with all the rigor and forms, which were afterwards imported and introduced into it by the Normans. The oppreſſive multiplicity of tenures and other feudal conſequences, which were never completely aboliſhed till the days of King Charles the Second, were abuſive emanations of an original principle

 of

of ſimplicity and liberty, to which if we recur, and upon it revive, or even introduce an uſage congenial with the preſent times, manners, and circumſtances, a ſhadow of imputation cannot lie againſt us of attempting to alter the law or infringe the conſtitution.

*The free Power of aliening Land in a commercial Country.*

The experience of many centuries has moſt incontrovertibly proved, that the free power of aliening land, with certain modifications and reſtrictions, is eſſentially requiſite in a commercial country; and in this power of alienation, is moſt cloſely interwoven the neceſſary notoriety of the landowner's title. Lord Mansfield, in a learned and elaborate argument upon the nature of a diſſeiſin, in *Taylor* v. *Horde* (*a*), ſays, that " the different ſta-" tutes, which had given free liberty of alienation, " and aboliſhed all military tenures, had left us little " but the names of feoffment, ſeiſin, tenure, and " freeholder, without any preciſe knowledge of the " thing originally ſignified by theſe ſounds. Co-" pyholds, and the cuſtomary freeholds in the " North, retain faint traces, in imitation of the old " ſyſtem of feudal tenures. It is obvious, how a " man may viſibly be the copyholder or cuſtomary " freeholder *de facto*, in prejudice of the rightful " tenant; and it then was as notorious, who was " the feudal tenant *de facto*, as who now is *de facto* " incumbent of a living or mayor of a corpora-" tion."

(*a*) 1 Burr. p. 108.

*Notoriety*

*Notoriety of the firſt Acts of Alienation of Land.*

When this free power of alienation had once gained footing, the moſt ſolemn notoriety attended every act of alienation: the firſt mode of transferring landed property was, in the unlettered days of our warlike anceſtors, by the corporal tradition and inveſtiture in poſſeſſion of the aliened lands; and this was done with the utmoſt ſolemnity, *coram paribus de vicineto*; or it was rendered public and notorious by ſome other ſymbolical gift or tradition: (*a*) "At firſt many lands and eſtates were collated or "beſtowed by bare word of mouth, without writing "or charter, only with the lord's ſword or helmet, or "a horn or a cup; and very many times with a ſpur, "with a currycomb, with a bow, and ſome with an "arrow: but theſe things were in the beginning of "the Norman reign: in after times this faſhion was "altered." But as in proceſs of time, great inconveniences were experienced from the evidence of titles reſting ſolely upon the perſonal memory of the witneſſes to ſuch acts of alienation, written conveyances were introduced; the firſt form of which was the deed of feoffment: and although the words of the deed, which in fact was a tranſaction only between the grantor and grantee, contained the nature of the transfer, and the duration of the eſtate intended to be thereby given; yet the feoffment, or rather the transfer or alienation, was not perfected till the *livery of ſeiſin*, which was made *coram paribus de vicineto*, who indorſed upon the back of the deed of feoffment their atteſtation as to the manner, place, and time of ſuch livery. *Nam feudum ſine inveſtiturâ nullo modo conſtitui poteſt* (*b*);

(*a*) Selden's Janus Anglorum, c. 3. p. 54.
(*b*) Wright 37.

nor was the transfer or alienation complete, till, as Fleta (*a*) says, *fit juris et seisinæ conjunctio.*

So says Mr. Justice Blackstone: (*b*) "Livery "of seisin, by the common law, is necessary to be "made upon every grant of an estate of freehold "in hereditaments corporeal, whether of inheri-"tance or for life only: and in leases for years, an "actual entry is necessary to vest the estate in the "lessee; for the bare lease gives him only a right "to enter, which is called his interest in the term, "or *interesse termini*; and when he enters in pur-"suance of that right, he is then, and not before, "in possession of his term, and complete tenant "for years. This entry by the tenant himself "served the purpose of notoriety, as well as livery "of seisin from the grantor could have done. Thus "is it observable, how upon the old principles "the modern rules of law are grounded; for, even "to this day, you cannot grant a freehold to com-"mence *in futuro:* the reason is, that at common "law such a grant could not be made without li-"very of seisin; and this livery being an actual "tradition of the land, must take effect *in presenti*, "or not at all."

It is obvious, that there can be no livery of seisin of incorporeal hereditaments, or of such things as, by lawyers, are said to lie in grant; as advowsons, commons, rents, seignories, reversions, &c.: *Res incorporales, quæ sunt ipsum jus rei, vel corpori inhærens traditionem non patiuntur.* (*c*) Therefore, as Mr. Justice Blackstone further observes, "These "things passed merely by the delivery of the "deed; but then such grant, together with the "attornment of the tenant, were held to be of

(*a*) Fleta 2. l. 3. c. 15. § 5.
(*b*) Blackst. Com. vol. 2. p. 314.
(*c*) Bracton, l. 2. c. 18.

" equal notoriety with, and therefore equivalent to " a feoffment and livery of lands in immediate " possession (*a*)."

As early then, as landed property could be transferred or aliened by deed, we trace this first essential principle; that the utmost notoriety always attended the act of alienation. And although in process of time, either by the arts or inattention of conveyancers, modes have been devised and established of passing lands in a very secret manner, yet it certainly never could have been the intention nor spirit of that law, which, as we have seen, required such determined notoriety in every act of alienation of land. This want of notoriety has frequently been a subject of discussion, both to lawyers and statesmen: and it is therefore no less astonishing than true, that the subject has never been thoroughly investigated, and consequently neither faithfully represented nor properly understood. The further enquiry into it at present shall be introduced in Mr. Justice Blackstone's words (*b*).

" In the ancient feudal method of conveyance, " (by giving corporeal seisin of the lands) this no- " toriety was in some measure answered; but all " the advantages resulting from thence are now " totally defeated by the introduction of death-bed " devises and secret conveyances; and there has " never yet been any sufficient guard against frau- " dulent charges and incumbrances: since the dis- " use of the old Saxon custom of transacting all " conveyances at the county court, and entering a " memorial of them in the chartulary or leger " book of some adjacent monastery, and the failure " of the general register established by King

(*a*) Blackst. 2 v. c. 20. p. 317.
(*b*) Blackst. 2 vol. c. 20. p. 343.

" Richard

" Richard the firſt, for the ſtarrs (*a*) or mortgages
" made to Jews, in the *Capitulâ de Judeis*, (*b*) of
" which Hoveden has preſerved a copy. How far
" the eſtabliſhment of a like general regiſter for
" deeds and wills, and other acts affecting real
" property, would remedy this inconvenience, de-
" ſerves well to be conſidered. In Scotland, every
" act regarding the tranſmiſſion of property is re-
" gularly entered on record; and ſome of our own
" provincial diviſions, particularly the extended
" county of York and the populous county of
" Middleſex, have prevailed with the legiſlature to
" erect ſuch regiſters in their reſpective diſtricts."

In Ireland alſo, all deeds affecting lands are regiſtered, by which notoriety of the incumbrances, many important objections againſt lending money upon mortgage in that kingdom, are done away. From very frequent enquiries into the nature and conſequences of inrolling deeds in Scotland, and

(*a*) The Hebrew word *ſhetar* ſignifies a deed or contract: if therefore the firſt ſyllable be abbreviated, or rather if the whole word be contracted into one ſyllable, we ſhall have the ſound, by which a modern Northern Jew would pronounce the word *ſtar*. Hence it is more probable, that the *Star* Chamber was ſo called, than from its ſtarry cieling.

(*b*) It would be ill judged indeed to draw a line of parity between the reaſons for inrolling deeds and wills in the preſent age, and thoſe, which induced government in the 11th century to paſs theſe laws relating to the Jews: when we reflect, that they were paſſed in an age, when either the Jews would, or Chriſtians could otherwiſe believe, that they would yearly, on Good Friday, crucify a child of Chriſtian parents, in deriſion of the crucifixion of our bleſſed Redeemer. (Molloy, l. 3.) However, upon the general principle of avoiding cavilling and differences between adverſe parties, " every Jew was made to " ſwear upon his roll, that all his debts, and pawns and rents, " and all his goods and poſſeſſions he ſhould cauſe to be in- " rolled, and that he ſhould conceal nothing," &c. &c. It is a vulgar axiom, " believe every man honeſt, but deal with him, as if he were otherwiſe:" many hold this good as to individuals, but all muſt think it holds good as to legiſlative bodies.

registering them in Ireland, I have not found, that in any one instance, any reasonable complaint had ever been made either against the usage or the effects: on the contrary, I have observed much good thereby produced and felt (*a*).

In support of these ideas, it is very satisfactory to find, they are not new: in the preface to Baron Gilbert's learned Treatise of Tenures, it is said, "He has clearly explained the reason of those pub-
"lic ceremonies and acts of notoriety, required
"by the feudal law, for the acquiring, possessing,
"and transferring of feuds, and which formerly
"were equally requisite in our common law te-
"nures, viz. liveries, attornments, &c.; the disuse
"whereof has not only occasioned an uncertainty
"in many titles and estates, but also introduced
"that mischievous practice of private and secret
"feoffments, by lease and release, covenants to
"uses, &c. and which, in consequence, has intro-
"duced a deluge of perjuries, forgeries, and other
"corruptions over the common law, and which
"can never be rectified, or the mischief redressed,
"till the common law be, in that particular, res-
"tored to the ancient method of passing estates *in*
"*pais*, or by some public act of notoriety."

*Popular Prejudices not to be disregarded.*

I do not think, that popular prejudices are always justly grounded, and reasonably entertained; but they seldom subsist without some reason, that is *ad captum vulgi*, and within the ready apprehen-

(*a*) There has always appeared to me much more order reason and judgment, in all legal transactions in Scotland, than in Ireland: nor, in my opinion, can there be a more marked instance of that superiority, than in the inrolment, instead of the registry of deeds. I shall speak more fully hereafter of the very essential defects and mischiefs of the mutilated memorials of registered deeds in this kingdom.

sion

fion of the community. Thus it is well known, that in the purchafe of landed eftates, and much more in the negociations for the loan of money upon mortgage, or by way of annuity or rent charge, a decided preference is generally given to fecurities in the regiftering counties over thofe, in which no regiftry is eftablifhed: and for what reafon? but becaufe generally there is more confidence between the buyer and feller, and the lender and borrower, when the lands lie in a regiftering county, than when they lie in other places; and the lands are there found to be more marketable and negociable. And what can fo effectually raife the price and value of them, as this defirable quality? What can fo materially promote the trade of a country, as the eafe and fecurity, with which the merchant may inveft his gains in the purchafe of real property or land? What can fo effentially raife the value of land to the owner, as the facility, with which he can render it fubfervient to every purpofe of providing for his family, relieving his diftreffes, or even gratifying his pleafures and inclinations? Thefe again are no new ideas: A fmall pamphlet publifhed in the year 1696, intituled, *A Propofal for the erecting County Regifters for Freehold Lands, fhewing the great Ufe and Benefit of them*, has thefe words, "It is the cheapnefs and facility of procur-" ing money, that is the benefit defigned to the " borrower, as certainty and fecurity is to the " lender. If we gain thefe two points, the principal " benefit of land is gained, which is to make them " funds for carrying on the trade of the nation, to " the public and private benefit." The vulgar prejudice then in favour of the regiftering counties, is grounded upon thefe plaufible reafons; that thereby the value of the land is increafed to the owner, by its becoming more negociable and marketable; and titles and fecurities become thereby by more clear and unobjectionable to the monied men for investing their money in purchases or mortgages. Plausible as these reasons are, we are now to examine how far they are just and actually exist.

In the sequel of my researches, I am happy in moving upon a principle, which evidently is founded in the ancient laws of this country; and that much experience may be called in to the aid of my argument, not only from our sister kingdoms, but also, in a very great measure, from our own. We have seen, that the first method of conveying land by a written deed, was done with the greatest publicity and notoriety; and therefore, after such a conveyance, there was not supposed to remain any secret title or suppressed right in any other. The person, to whom such conveyance was thus publicly and notoriously made, was supposed to acquire thereby such a right, as he could maintain against all men (*a*). "By the ancient feudal law, no "man could alien without a licence from the lord "of the fee, and this licence was part of the no-"toriety on such alienations. And if they alie-"nated without such licence, the feud was for-"feited. Nor could the lords part with their ma-"nors and services without the attornment of "their tenants, &c." But we are now gone by the time, when, as Lord Bacon says (*b*), "all "inheritances could not pass, but by acts overt and "notorious, as by deeds *livery and records*." And it must be the conviction of every person, who turns a thought to the subject, that as the occasions of charging and selling lands are become now more frequent, than they have heretofore been, it is become now therefore more requisite than ever, I

(*a*) Gilb. Tenures of continual Claim, p. 46.
(*b*) Bac. reading on the Statute of Uses, p. 329.

do

do not ſay to alter or new model the forms of conveyances and alienations of lands, but rather to reſtore them to their ancient mode and principle.

*Proofs of the ancient Notoriety in the Alienation of Lands.*

There is no higher authority than the ſtatutes of the realm, both as to the law, which they enact; as to the uſages and practices, which they recite. I ſhall therefore upon this principle, quote the firſt words of the preamble of the famous ſtatute of uſes, paſſed in the 27th year of the reign of King Henry VIII. (A. D. 1535), of which Lord Bacon ſays (*a*), it is a law " whereupon the inheritances " of this realm are toſſed at this day like a ſhip " upon the ſea (*b*)." " Where, by the common law " of this realm, lands, tenements and hereditaments " be not deviſable by teſtament, nor ought to be " transferred from one to another, but by ſolemn " livery and ſeiſin, matter of record, writing ſuffi- " cient made *bonâ fide*, without covin or fraud; " yet nevertheleſs divers and ſundry imaginations, " ſubtle inventions and practices have been uſed, " whereby the hereditaments of this realm have " been conveyed from one to another by frau- " dulent feoffments, fines, recoveries, and other aſ- " ſurances craftily made to ſecret uſes, intents and " truſts; and alſo by wills and teſtaments ſome " time made by nude parolx and words, ſome " time by ſigns and tokens, and ſome time by " writing," &c. &c. Then reciting ſeveral miſchiefs produced thereby, " *to the utter ſubverſion of* " *the ancient common laws of this realm*," the pre-

(*a*) Bacon's reading upon this ſtatute, p. 12.
(*b*) 27th H. VIII. c. 10.

amble concludes, "For the extirping and extinguishment of all ſuch ſubtle practiſed feoffments, "fines, recoveries, abuſes, and errors heretofore "uſed and accuſtomed in this realm, to the ſubverſion of the good and ancient laws of the ſame; "and to the intent, that the King's Highneſs, or "any other his ſubjects of this realm, ſhall not, "in anywiſe hereafter, by any means or inventions, "be deceived, damaged, or hurt, by reaſon of ſuch "truſts, uſes or confidences," &c. And it then enacts, with very great propriety, that *the uſe of the land ſhall be ever coupled with the poſſeſſion*; thus endeavouring to reſtore the purity and ſimplicity of the common law of alienation or transfer of land.

## *Of Uſes.*

In order to evade the ſtatute of mortmain, and afterwards to cloak and preſerve property from confiſcations, in the contentions between the houſes of York and Lancaſter, the doctrine of Uſes was introduced, countenanced and eſtabliſhed; and upon the ſubtilty of veſting the uſe of the land in one perſon, and retaining the poſſeſſion of it in another, the plain honourable civil purpoſes of the common and ſtatute laws of this realm were defeated; and a labyrinth of abſtruſe doctrine was eſtabliſhed and monopolized by the then profeſſors of the law, whoſe ungenerous principle was to keep their clients in all poſſible ignorance, that they might reap an unfair advantage from the miſchievous ſubtleties, they had artfully introduced.

After this ſtatute had paſſed, the parliament in the ſame ſeſſion found it adviſeable to enact, that the only method, by which it was then known, that a freehold could be transferred indiſcriminately from man to man, (and which had ariſen out of the

the doctrine of uſes) which was by bargain and ſale for a pecuniary conſideration, ſhould retain ſome notoriety or publication, equivalent at leaſt to that of a feoffment with livery and ſeiſin. So Lord Bacon (*a*): "But the parliament, that made "that ſtatute, did foreſee, that it would be miſ- "chievous, that men's lands ſhould ſo ſuddenly, "upon the payment of a little money, be con- "veyed from them, peradventure in an alehouſe "or in a tavern, upon ſtrainable advantages; did "therefore gravely provide another act in the ſame "parliament, that the land, upon payment of this "money, ſhould not paſs away, except there were "a writing indented made between the ſaid two "parties, and the ſaid writing alſo within ſix "months inrolled in ſome of the courts of Weſt- "minſter, or in the ſeſſions rolls in the ſhire, "where the land lieth, unleſs it be in the cities "or corporate towns, where they did uſe to "inroll deeds; and there the ſtatute extendeth "not" (*b*).

*Reaſons of ſome Deeds not being inrolled.*

Another mode of conveyance ſprung out of this wily doctrine of uſes, which, becauſe the conſider- ation of ſuch deed neceſſarily was marriage or conſanguinity, it was not perhaps thought by the legiſlature open to ſuch fraud nor deceit; and as it did not paſs the land out of the owner's family, it might not require the ſame degree of notoriety and

(*a*) Uſe of the Law, p. 150.

(*b*) The particular cuſtoms of inrolling deeds in ſome towns and corporations, may fairly be preſumed to have been adopted and eſtabliſhed, upon the idea of a more frequent circulation of property in the place where the cuſtom prevailed; or that it was a relict of an univerſal uſage throughout the nation, retain- ed in particular places: both which reaſons ſtrongly enforce the neceſſity of an univerſal inrolment.

publication;

publication; and therefore such a deed, which is called a *covenant to stand seised to uses*, needs not to be inrolled. Lord Bacon (*a*) speaks of it, as follows. "A man that hath a wife and children, being "king'sfolks, may by writing under his hand "and seal agree, that for their or any of their "preferment he will stand seised of his lands to "their uses, either in tail or fee, so as he shall see "cause: upon which agreement in writing, there "ariseth an equity or honesty, that the lands should "go according to those agreements; nature and "reason allowing these provisions, of which equi-"ty and honesty is the use, and the use being cre-"ated in this sort, the statute of 27 H. VIII. "before mentioned conveyeth the estate of the "land (*b*), as the use is appointed. And so this "covenant to stand seised to uses is at this day, "since the said statute, a conveyance of land; and "with this difference from a bargain and sale, in that "this needeth no inrolment, as a bargain and sale "doth, nor needeth not to be in writing indented, "as a bargain and sale must: and if the party, "to whose use he agreeth to stand seised of the "land, be not wife or child, cousin, or one, that he "meaneth to marry, then will no use rise, and so "no conveyance."

Without departing from the time, of which Lord Bacon speaks, all other assurances of land then in usage were, as the same still are, made by matter of record; and consequently with that species of notoriety, which I am endeavouring to shew, ought to attend every deed and will affecting land.

Mr. Justice Blackstone says (*c*), "Assurances

(*a*) Bac. ubi supra, p. 151.

(*b*) *i. e.* by coupling the use with the possession, or transferring the use into possession.

(*c*) Black. Com. Vol. II. l. 2. c. 21.

" by matter of record call in the ſanction of a " court of record to ſubſtantiate, preſerve, and be " a perpetual teſtimony of the transferring of pro- " perty from one man to another, or of its eſtabliſh- " ment when already transferred. Of this nature " are, 1°, Private acts of parliament; 2°, The " king's grants; 3°, Fines; 4°, Common reco- " veries." It would exceed the intention of my deſign, to explain the nature of theſe four modes of affecting landed property: ſuffice it to ſay, what every one knows, that they are methods, by which a title to land may be acquired, or by which the land may be affected; and that not one of them can be practiſed without the moſt ſolemn and public notoriety.

*Deductions.*

If it be expedient to render public and notorious the act, by which the moſt ſure and ſolid title to land is acquired; it muſt be for ſome reaſons, which enforce that expediency: whatever reaſons theſe are, they muſt eſſentially counteract the propriety or expediency of any title to land being acquired without ſuch notoriety; for *a majore ad minus valet conſequentia.* If the king in perſon, who is not preſumed to err; if his judges in court, whoſe judgment is mandatory; if the legiſlative body, whoſe authority is uncontroulable, cannot transfer land, or give title unto it without the ſolemnity of publicity, notoriety, and perpetuity, *a fortiori,* individuals, whoſe judgment is always fallible, whoſe integrity is often ſuſpicious, whoſe artifices are ſometimes refined and almoſt impenetrable, ought not to be permitted to transfer land or give title unto it, without at leaſt equal publicity, notoriety, and perpetuity.

When the legiſlature in the 27th year of King Henry

Henry VIII. enacted, that *every bargain and ſale of lands ſhould be by deed indented and inrolled,* there was no other method or form known or practiſed of ſelling or transferring land, (except by deed of feoffment with livery and ſeiſin). And indeed this deed of bargain and ſale itſelf was a novelty introduced into the law, together with or ſpringing out of the doctrine of uſes. And I may here properly again ſay with Judge Blackſtone (*a*), " It is impracticable, upon our preſent plan, to pur-" ſue the doctrine of uſes through all the refine-" ments and niceties, which the ingenuity of the " times, (abounding in ſubtle diſquiſitions) deduced " from this child of the imagination, when once a " departure was permitted from the plain ſimple " rules of property eſtabliſhed by the ancient law."

As theſe ſubtle inventions and innovations had for centuries been weaving themſelves into the texture of the law, and thus had become, as it were, of a piece with the law itſelf, it was difficult for parliament to deviſe at once a remedy perfectly commenſurate with the miſchief, without perhaps venturing upon the too hazardous experiment, of aboliſhing the whole ſyſtem, with all its mediate and immediate conſequences.

*Lands deviſeable.*

From the change of laws introduced by the Normans, to the days of Henry VIII. lands were not deviſeable, which was found by experience to be inconvenient; though by ſpecial cuſtom, as in London and elſewhere, lands might be given by wills; and this was a relict of the Saxon liberties or laws, by which lands were deviſeable. Upon this doctrine of uſes then, a perſon wiſhing his land

(*a*) Black. Com. Vol. II. c. 20. p. 33.

after his death to go in a different ſucceſſion from the deſcent, which the law would have caſt it in, conveyed during his life his land to a friend in truſt; and then by his will would declare how his friend ſhould diſpoſe of it. This declaration by will raiſed *an uſe*, which gave the benefits and profits of the land to the perſon intended to be benefited by the will, whilſt the land itſelf was legally and really veſted in the perſon, to whom it had been conveyed, and to whom livery and ſeiſin had been made; and he was called the feoffee in truſt. But the ſtatute of uſes, which transferred the uſe into poſſeſſion, neceſſarily defeated this ſhifting evaſion of the law; for after this ſtatute, the raiſing of *an uſe* in land was giving the real poſſeſſion of the land; and this would have been to all intents and purpoſes a deviſe of lands, which ever ſince the introduction, or rather the new modelling of the feudal ſyſtem by the Normans, had not been allowed. It was however ſoon found expedient to alter the law in this regard; and by the 32d of Henry VIII. perſons were enabled to give and deviſe lands by will, under certain reſtrictions.

Here parliament, as in many other inſtances, changing the ancient law or remedying an evil, was inattentive to one of the moſt material conſequences of ſuch innovation; which was, to provide for the ſolemnity and notoriety of that act, by which land is given to a ſtranger, and the right heir, whom the law ever favors and protects, is diſinherited and deprived or defeated of his legal rights, in a manner certainly more liable to deceit, fraud, art and undue influence, than any act or deed, which operates and takes its full effect, during the lifetime of the grantor or donor. But of this want of notoriety in wills of land, I ſhall ſpeak more fully hereafter.

*Intro-*

*Introduction of ſecret Conveyances.*

In proceſs of time, ſtill upon this doctrine of uſes, the ingenuity of conveyancers, and particularly of Sir Orlando Bridgman, before whom more than two thirds of the titles in the kingdom, after the civil wars, had been laid or ſubmitted, introduced a new mode of conveyance, to which (for reaſons never publicly given, for they would not ſtand the teſt of public inveſtigation and judgment) they gave the full effects of feoffment with livery and ſeiſin, or bargain and ſale inrolled; but without the notoriety either of the one or of the other. This was a conveyance by *leaſe and releaſe*, which is now become the moſt common conveyance of lands. For in the doctrine of uſes, a very ſtrange and unaccountable rule of law had prevailed and been eſtabliſhed, viz. that *no uſe could be limited on an uſe*; (*a*) by which it was underſtood, that, if A. for money bargained and ſold his land to B. it raiſed an uſe in the land to B. which uſe being transferred into poſſeſſion by the ſtatute of uſes, no further limitation could be engrafted upon it. Now it often happens, that there is occaſion to limit lands to A. and his heirs, to the uſe of ſeveral different perſons in remainder, and for different eſtates; to ſome for life, to others in tail, either male or female; and to another in fee, as is uſually the caſe in marriage-ſettlements. For example, the owner of the land generally conveys it by leaſe and releaſe to two truſtees, (who are called the releaſees to uſes and truſtees of the inheritance to preſerve the contingent remainders, &c.) to the uſe of him-ſelf for life, then to the uſe of the truſtees to ſerve the contingent remainders from being feated, but to hold it in truſt for the tenant

(*a*) Dyer 155.

 life;

life; then to the ufe and intent of providing a jointure for the intended wife, or to her for life in like manner as to himfelf; then to the ufe of other truftees for a term of years, for the purpofes of better fecuring the jointure and providing portions and maintenances for the younger children; then to the iffue of the marriage in tail, with perhaps feveral voluntary remainders to relations or friends; and the ultimate remainder to the fettler in fee-fimple.

All thefe different limitations could not be made by a bargain and fale inrolled, *becaufe an ufe cannot be limited upon an ufe.* So from this doctrine of ufes, various innovations have at different times been introduced into the practice of conveyancing: but as the principles, upon which thefe innovations were grounded, were heterogeneous from thofe of the ancient law; fo no wonder, that the introductors of them loft fight of the leading features of the old law, which were notoriety and perpetuity, as we have feen in feoffments with livery and feifin, and bargains and fales inrolled. It would exceed the extent of my plan, and be irrelevant to the fubject under confideration, to enter more fully into the nature, operation, and effects of a conveyance by leafe and releafe: fuffice it to have faid, that by the general law of this country, they need not now be inrolled, no more than wills or any other private conveyances of land, (except bargains and fales for a pecuniary confideration.)

## *Further Proofs of the ancient Notoriety of all Deeds affecting Lands.*

Copyhold eftates are nothing more nor lefs, than certain cuftoms or ufages, which, though formerly general and common to other lands, have by particular

ticular privilege, grant, or even chance, been retained and preserved in different manors, after the general tenure of lands throughout the kingdom was altered and changed. Although many of these customs vary in different manors, yet there is one principal usage, which is, I believe, universally and unexceptionably common to every manor, in which any copyhold customs or usages are preserved. And this is, that no copyholder (or tenant holding by copy of court roll) shall or may pass away, change, alter, or affect his land, without making this deed or act in some shape notorious in the manor court. Nothing so strongly proves an ancient usage, as the preservation of it in particular subordinate jurisdictions: and there is no method so sure of proving the existence of a law or usage, as to shew that parliament has taken its benefits or abuses into consideration. So early then as in the year 1384 (*a*) "at the complaint of the said commonalty made "to the lord the king in the parliament, for that "great disherison" (*exheredatio*, or loss of the right heir's title) "in times past was done (or happened) to the people, and may be done, by the false "*entering of pleas, rasing of rolls, and changing of* "*verdicts, &c.* it is accorded and assented, that if "any judge or clerk be of such default, so that "by the same default there ensueth disinherison of "any of the parties, &c. &c. he shall be punished by fine and ransom at the king's will "and satisfy the party." Can any thing more conclusively evince, that in those days the deeds and muniments to men's estates were inrolled and recorded, that is, rendered public, notorious, and perpetual? I now hope I have said enough to prove, that the requisition of notoriety and perpetuity to every act, by which land is affected, is

(*a*) 8 Ric. 2. c. 4.

congenial with the principles of the ancient law, and therefore that it ought to be univerſally eſtabliſhed throughout the kingdom.

*It is more neceſſary in the preſent, than in any paſt Age, to render every Act, by which Land is affected, public, notorious, and perpetual.*

In the reign of Queen Elizabeth, a motion was made in the houſe of commons for leave to bring in a bill to prohibit uſury; by which nothing more in thoſe days was meant, than placing out money at intereſt: for it is ſince the regulating of the rate of intereſt, that the word *uſury* has been appropriated to every illegal exceſs of that rate. A great ſtateſman then in the houſe oppoſed it, and concluded his argument for the continuance of it, with this memorable aphoriſm: *Let any man ſhew me a country without uſury, and I will ſhew him one without trade or riches:* than the truth of which, nothing is more clear nor certain. As then the facility of borrowing money upon reaſonable intereſt, is eſſential to the trade and commerce of a country; ſo it follows, that the more certain and ſatisfactory the ſecurity is, upon which the money borrowed is placed out, the more conducive is it to the lending and borrowing: and by how much more uſeful and ſubſervient to theſe ends the land is rendered, by ſo much will its value and price be raiſed; and there needs no argument to prove, that by the value and price of land, the national funds muſt riſe and fall; and their fluctuation is the true and juſt barometer of the credit and proſperity of the nation. It neceſſarily follows, that whatever raiſes the value and price of land, muſt alſo increaſe the price of ſtock, and conſequently tend to promote the credit and proſperity of the kingdom. Upon the ſame prin-

ciple

ciple will it appear, that in proportion to the difficulties of raiſing money, muſt the circulation of property be checked; and the free circulation of property is evidently eſſential to the flouriſhing ſtate of a commercial country. A title to land becomes more complicated, abſtruſe, and difficult, in proportion to the number, variety, and intricacy of deeds, through which it is deduced. If that notoriety, which was required by the ancient law, had attended every transfer of landed property, much intricacy and uncertainty in titles would have been avoided: but we muſt argue, as well as judge from facts. The free power of alienation, the flouriſhing ſtate of trade, the increaſe of wealth in circulation, the accumulation of ſtatutes, judgments, and decrees reſpecting the rights and titles of land-owners, the ignorance of many, who undertake to practiſe as conveyancers, the refinement of ſome, and the diffuſe prolixity of almoſt all practitioners, muſt ever tend to increaſe the intricacy and uncertainty of the land-owner's title to his eſtates. Now upon the admiſſion of the principle, that the circulation of property muſt ever be in proportion to the extent of trade, we muſt infer, that as the trade of this country never was ſo extenſive, as in the preſent hour, and conſequently luxury and refinement (from which it will be difficult to abſtract extravagance and diſſipation) never were ſo prevalent in this country, as at preſent, ſo therefore never were there ſo many occaſions and calls for money by the diſtreſſed, or for ſecurities by the affluent. What then follows? At no period was it ſo neceſſary and expedient, for the good of commerce and proſperity of the nation, that the loan of money upon land ſhould meet with few obſtructions and difficulties.

If theſe incidental reaſons did not ſubſiſt, yet there

there are demonſtrative arguments in favour of my opinion; for it is uncontrovertable, that all future purchaſers and mortgagees muſt eſſentially find their titles, if not more difficult, at leaſt more prolix, and conſequently open to more perplexity, doubt and defect, than the perſons, under or through whom they claim: for, to whatever before exiſted, they ſuperadd the chances of a new negotiation being affected by ſome omiſſion, flaw, inefficacy or fraud. How neceſſary then it is, that a counterpoiſe ſhould be thrown into the ſcale againſt an evil ſo pernicious in its effects! And what can anſwer that purpoſe ſo effectually, as ſecuring notoriety and perpetuity to the titles of every deſcription of land, ſo that purchaſers and incumbrancers may read their own titles upon the face of the records?

I ſhall aſſuredly meet credit when I ſay, or rather repeat, that every reaſon for eſtabliſhing an univerſal inrolment acquires accumulated ſtrength by proceſs of time; and it is now a full century, ſince Sir Matthew Hale wrote a *treatiſe, ſhewing how uſeful, ſafe, reaſonable, and beneficial the inroling and regiſtering of all conveyances of lands may be to the inhabitants of this kingdom*; in which he ſets out with enumerating the miſchiefs propounded to be remedied, which are: " 1ſt. The " great deceit committed by perſons of ſecret judg- " ments, mortgages, conveyances and ſettlements, " whereby purchaſers are oftentimes deceived and " creditors defeated: and this the more conſider- " able in England, becauſe indeed the great inland " trade we have, is the trade of buying and ſell- " ing of lands; and the great ſecurity, that is " ordinarily given to creditors and lenders of mo- " ney, is by ſecurity of land. 2. The multitude " of chargeable and difficult ſuits in law occa-

" ſioned

"sioned by preconveyances, which probably would "be avoided and lessened, if all men's estates lay "open to the view of others."

It must be remarked, that Sir Matthew Hale wrote this treatise many years before any of the registries were established in any of the three ridings of the county of York or in the county of Middlesex; that he talks indiscriminately of inrolment and registry, which are in fact very materially different; that he had not felt the experience of either: nor had he the happiness to see the trade of his country flourish in any degree, comparative with its present state.

## *Parliamentary Redress of Grievances.*

It is no less true than wonderful, that when an abuse or mischief is felt, the party aggrieved, having no legal nor equitable remedy, or perhaps being unwilling to hazard the expence of an action or suit, uncertain and doubtful in its issue, applies to some person in parliament for redress of the grievance. The matter originated in a particular case, and a bill is brought in to obviate or prevent the mischief; the origin, progress, and effect of which, were never submitted to the consideration of those, who were competent to see and correct and prevent the mischief: but parliament, generally inclined to check evil and promote good, gives credit to those, who undertake to bring in the bill, which tends to these general ends, not only for their laudable intentions, but also for their having fully considered and devised the proper and effectual means of attaining the ends proposed by the bill. Thus when, in the year 1692 (*a*), an act passed *to prevent frauds by clandestine mortgages,*

(*a*) 4 & 5 William and Mary, c. 16.

it

it was a thing, to which no oppoſition could be given: and it is well known, how few members of either houſe are, or I preſume then were, competent to judge of the ſubject; and the few profeſſional members in the houſe might not take any active part in the bill, unleſs profeſſionally or officially engaged in the paſſing of it.

Let us conſider firſt the preamble of this act: "Whereas great frauds and deceits are too often "practiſed by neceſſitous and evil-diſpoſed perſons, "in borrowing of money, and giving judgments, "ſtatutes, and recognizances privately, for ſecur-"ing the repayment of the ſaid money; and the "ſame perſons do afterwards borrow money upon "ſecurity of their lands of other perſons, and do "not acquaint the latter lender thereof with the "ſame, whereby ſuch late lender is very often in "danger to loſe his whole money, or forced to pay "off the debts ſecured by the ſaid judgments, "ſtatutes, and recognizances, before they can "have any benefit of the ſaid mortgages: And "whereas divers perſons do many times mort-"gage their lands more than once, without giving "notice of their firſt mortgage, whereby lenders "of money upon ſecond or after-mortgages do "often loſe their money, and are put to great "charges in ſuits and otherwiſe," &c.

The firſt queſtion I aſk upon this, is, What is meant by giving *judgments, ſtatutes, and recognizances privately?* No judgment acknowledged for debt hath effect, or is in fact a judgment, till entered up in public court, and thereby made public and notorious to all mankind. Statutes are either *merchant* or of *the ſtaple* (*a*): a *ſtatute merchant* is a bond of *record*, acknowledged before the clerk of the ſtatutes merchant and the lord-mayor of the

(*a*) Terms de Ley 548.

city

city of London, or two merchants aſſigned for that purpoſe, and before the mayors of other cities and towns, or the bailiffs of any boroughs, and ſealed with the ſeal of the debtor and the king, upon condition, that if the obligor pays not the debt at the day, execution may be awarded againſt his body, lands, and goods, and the obligee ſhall hold the lands to him and his heirs till the debt be levied. (*a*) *Statutes ſtaple* are concerning merchants and merchandizes of the ſtaple, and of the ſame nature with *ſtatutes merchant:* they are for debt acknowledged before the mayor of the ſtaple, at our chief cities, &c. in the preſence of one or more of the conſtables of the ſtaple, by virtue of which, the creditor may forthwith have execution of the body, lands, and goods of the debtor on nonpayment. A *recognizance* is alſo a bond or obligation of record acknowledged to the king; and when for debt, is uſually taken and acknowledged before a judge or a magiſtrate. Every one of theſe ſecurities for money is eſſentially of public notoriety, and therefore cannot by poſſibility *be given privately*.

It certainly muſt appear ſtrange, that there ſhould exiſt a neceſſity of diſcloſing to a lender of money, what is a record of the court, and is open to the inſpection and knowledge of all the world. For what other reaſon can ſtatutes or judgments be entered of record in the court, unleſs for the prevention of ſecrecy and privacy? It is alſo ſingular, that when this preamble mentions *prior mortgages and other incumbrances*, which may well exiſt without the knowledge of any man, and remain for any length of time concealed and ſuppreſſed in impregnable ſecrecy, it ſeems to have loſt ſight of the very poſſibility of their being kept ſecret or private.

(*a*) 4 Inſtit. 238.

Upon

Upon confidering attentively the purport and tendency of this preamble, will not every man conclude, that the act will enfure fome preventive againft the fraud, by rendering the privacy and fecrecy of fuch clandeftine tranfactions impoffible, or provide fome effectual remedy to the lender, in cafe his fecurity be rendered null and void or ineffectual by fome fuch prior incumbrance? I do not find, in the Journals, upon whofe motion the bill was brought in: I fee, however, that Mr. Serjeant Trenchard was one of the committee, to whom it was referred, and that Mr. Waller reported feveral amendments made in the bill by the committee: however, fuch as it then paffed, fuch is the act at prefent, of which we are now to judge. It enacts, that any debtor upon judgment, ftatute or recognizance, taking up money upon mortgage, without having given notice of this debt upon the judgment, ftatute or recognizance to the mortgagee, fhall lofe his equity of redemption, and the mortgagee may from the execution of his mortgage deed (where no notice of this public debt upon record hath been given in writing), hold and enjoy the mortgaged lands for the eftate and term granted by the mortgage deed againft the mortgagor, and all claiming under him, as fully to all intents and purpofes whatfoever, as if the fame had been purchafed abfolutely, and without any power or liberty of redemption. And any perfon mortgaging the fame land more than once, without giving notice of the firft or prior mortgage, is in like manner deprived of all relief or equity of redemption againft the fecond or other mortgagee; and fuch fecond or after mortgagee fhall hold in like manner againft the mortgagor, and all claiming under him.

It is alfo enacted, that " if it fo happen that " there

" there be more than one mortgage at the ſame
" time made by any perſon or perſons to any per-
" ſon or perſons of the ſame lands and tenements,
" the ſeveral late or under mortgagees, his, her or
" their heirs, executors, adminiſtrators or aſſigns,
" ſhall have power to redeem any former mortgage
" or mortgages, upon payment of the principal
" debt, intereſt, and coſts of ſuit to the prior
" mortgagee or mortgagees, his, her or their
" heirs, executors, adminiſtrators or aſſigns, any
" thing herein contained to the contrary in anywiſe
" notwithſtanding."

As it is with a view to procure the repeal of this act, that I take it under my preſent conſideration, the freedom with which I muſt neceſſarily argue upon it, will not, I truſt, diſpleaſe nor offend. The remedy provided by this act for the evils ſet forth in the recital, is either frivolous and ineffectual, or it is unreaſonable and unjuſt; for either the prior incumbrance or debt, whether it be of record or by mortgage, is ſo large, as if paid off will leave little or no reſidue to the ſecondary mortgagee; or ſo ſmall, as if diſcharged the ſecondary mortgagee will retain a full and ample ſecurity for the money he has advanced. In the firſt caſe, to what end ſhall a mortgagor be hindered from redeeming lands which, if ſold, would not pay half the money advanced upon them? For redemption in this caſe would be purchaſing lands at double price, and a folly, of which a man ſo diſtreſſed or iniquitous, as to borrow money upon an inſufficient ſecurity, would never be ſuſpected; and then the remedy is frivolous and ineffectual. In the other caſe, I ſuppoſe a man having confeſſed and entered up a judgment for £. 1000, afterwards mortgages his lands (which are worth twenty times the ſum borrowed) for £. 2000: I will attribute the omiſſion to give the mortgagee notice of the judgment to his own ignorance, oblivion, inattention, or total reliance upon his law agent; or to the inexperience, inadvertency, or omiſſion of his law agent. There could be no intention of defrauding in the mortgagor; nor is there a poſſibility of the lender's loſing his money. And will any man find it reaſonable or equitable, that ſuch a mortgagor ſhould, in any poſſible caſe, be bound to pay more than the principal and intereſt of the money borrowed? Whereas by this act he would be not only compelled to pay the principal and intereſt, which he had borrowed, but alſo loſe the fee-ſimple of his eſtate worth twenty times the ſum borrowed, which in fact he had only pledged as a ſecurity for the repayment of the loan.

Let a perſon ſo liable to this ſtatute apply for relief, and who will not ſay that it would be unjuſt to refuſe it to him? If the execution of a law be unreaſonable and unjuſt, what obligation is there not upon the legiſlature to repeal it?

The act was undoubtedly meant to prevent fraud; whereas it is ſcarcely poſſible to open a door, through which more fraudulent impoſition and remedileſs iniquity can be let in, under the ſanction of parliamentary authority. I will not ſtate hypothetical poſſibilities, but real facts, which have repeatedly come within my own knowledge; and from them will I argue.

A gentleman of fortune, from play or other folly, wants a temporary ſum of money; he applies to one of that humane accommodating ſociety, who are ever ſanguine to relieve the diſtreſſes of inconſiderate youth. He grants an annuity, upon his own life, for ſix years purchaſe, and executes a bond and warrant of attorney, to confeſs a judgment upon the debt; and according to the terms of the advertiſement, which brought him hither, in the ſpace of an hour he is accommodated with the money. He pays, departs; and from ſhame or vexation, complies ſtrictly with another part of the advertiſement, which promiſes the moſt inviolable ſecrecy. The year comes round, and he finds the ſecond half yearly payment (for the firſt had been retained in advance) widely diſproportionate from the uſual rate of intereſt; and he accordingly applies to his regular law agent, to raiſe for him by mortgage as much money, as he wants to pay off this, and perhaps ſome other private debts. It rarely happens, that money advanced by advertiſement in this manner is claimed by the real owner. The link of advertiſers, runners and lenders, is ſeldom known. It ſo happens, that the lender of the ſecond ſum upon mortgage, is not ignorant of the annuity and judgment, though his knowledge of it cannot be legally proved againſt him; and he certainly will not ſearch the regiſter to find out an incumbrance, the legal ignorance of which, he has in contemplation to turn ſo much to his own advantage. The borrower intends immediately to redeem his annuity at any price; and, aſhamed of the tranſaction, continues to ſuppreſs the knowledge of it from his regular law agent. He executes the mortgage-deed, receives the money, and on the next day undertakes the application of it himſelf. The agent of the mortgagor, relying either upon the general conduct and management, or the ſpecial aſſurance of his client, that no judgment had been entered up by him, never thinks of adviſing him to give notice, of what he preſumes does not exiſt. In fact, the greater part of the profeſſion think it the buſineſs of the lender's agent, and not of the borrower's, to ſearch the regiſter for judgments. The annuity is redeemed, but no ſatisfaction is entered upon the judgment; the mortgagor, ſome time afterwards, reſolves upon matrimony, and means to clear his eſtate before he ſettles it; he accordingly gives notice to his mortgagee to receive his money. How ſurpriſing, but at the ſame time how remedileſs is the de-mand of the mortgagee to hold the eſtate, which is of conſiderable value, as abſolutely, as if he had purchaſed it; and why? Becauſe no notice had been given in writing of the judgment, that had been entered up for the firſt private debt, and which, alas! ſurvived the mortgage only by one day. It is, I believe, a true fact, that at this hour there are mortgages in this nation to the amount of ſome millions of money, in which above one half of the mortgagors may, under this ſtatute, be debarred from redemption; and if it were enforced, I know no remedy to ſuch crying injuſtice againſt the ex-preſs letter of a ſtatute in force. The ignorance of the unfair, and the integrity of the honeſt lenders of money, have hitherto prevented frauds and iniqui-ties from being practiſed under this ſtatute without end, as they would be without remedy.

When the act gives power to a ſecondary mort-gagee to redeem any former mortgage, upon paying principal, intereſt and coſts, the ſame difficulty ariſes upon the amplitude of the ſecurity, which I mentioned before. And if the prior mortgage be really clandeſtine and unknown, there can be no re-demption of it by a ſecondary mortgagee, as is evi-dent. And it is, as the law is now ſettled, in the power of an iniquitous mortgagor to defeat all meſne incumbrances, by creating an ulterior charge, and permitting ſuch laſt mortgagee to buy in the firſt incumbrance, (which hitherto we ſuppoſe him to have kept ſecret) and by thoſe means to acquire a priority for any ſum of money over thoſe ſecon-dary mortgagees, to whom the act gave a right to redeem the firſt mortgage. Is not this evidently to leave the juggle and power of defrauding in the hands of the mortgagor? For if there be ſeveral mortgagees, the laſt mortgagee having lent his mo-ney upon a valuable conſideration, and without no-

tice,

tice, may by purchasing in the first incumbrance, which carries with it the legal estate, protect himself against any mortgagee subsequent to the first and prior to the last (*a*): and it hath been holden, that a person is not bound to take notice of an incumbrance, because it is of record (*b*). It is self-evident, that the only effectual method of preventing fraud by clandestine mortgages, incumbrances, &c. is to take away the possible existence of any clandestine mortgage or incumbrance. And surely it can be no hardship, if a purchaser or mortgagee be bound to look to his own security, if nothing, which is not obviously open to inspection, can affect his purchase or mortgage: nor can there be any difficulty in such requisition, since in the plan proposed, no land in any county will by possibility, be liable to any charge or incumbrance, which may not be seen in the books regularly kept in each county, for a very trivial fee; and of which a short entry may not be also seen in the metropolis, as the grand mart of money negociations of every species.

## *Of Notice.*

In consequence of many suits instituted by purchasers and mortgagees, who after they had laid out their money, were disturbed in their possessions, or had their titles litigated on account of some prior claims, many decisions have been made, which have established a very nice and curious doctrine concerning notice, which may be either *express* and *actual*, or *implied* and *presumptive*. And these decisions bear very hard, in some cases, upon incumbrancers, whose primary object should ever be simplicity

(*a*) Chan. Ca. 21. Boovey and Shipwick; Churchill and Grove, Ch. Ca. 35. 1 Vern. 187, 188. 2 Vez. 573. Strange 240.

(*b*) Greswold and Marsham, 2 Chan. Ca. 170.

plicity in their title, and facility in maintaining it. Now all this doctrine will be wholly useless, if every deed and will affecting the land of a vendor or mortgagor, shall appear upon the face of the inrolment, to which the purchaser and mortgagee may have access: it will be then impossible, that there should be any occasion for notice; for every one will be presumed cognizant of whatever can by possibility affect his purchase or security, provided it be within the reach of his own knowledge. But as the law is now supposed to be, and is laid down as settled by the modern writers, an incumbrance being of record, a purchaser is *not* bound to take notice of it, at his peril: it must be proved that he had *express notice*, in order for him to obtain relief, which the record is not (*a*).

Whatever may be the law at present of a record's not being sufficient notice of itself, it is no new nor unreasonable idea, that the inrolment of a deed should of itself be full and express notice to all those, whom the effect of the deed may concern. Thus by an act, which (*b*) was passed for regulating proceedings in the court of King's Bench at Westminster, it was enacted, "That no corpo-"ration, lord or lords of manors, or other person "or persons having grants by charter or other "good conveyances, who have inrolled, and have "had the same allowed in and by the said court, "shall hereafter be compelled to plead the same "to any inquisition returned by any coroner:" And why? Because the notoriety of inrolment may be known to all, and ought to be noticed by those, whom it concerns. The act imposes a penalty of 5*l.* upon any clerk of the crown, who shall issue any process against a party, who has in-

(*a*) Gresswold and Marsham, 2 Chancery Cases, 170.
(*b*) 4 & 5 Will. and Mary, c. 22.

rolled

rolled his title, and exempts him from it if it be not inrolled, for the reaſon given in the act, as follows: "And whereas divers perſons having grants "of felons goods and deodands, and inrolled and "pleaded as aforeſaid, do many times alien and "convey their intereſt therein to other perſon or "perſons, or by their laſt wills do deviſe the ſame, "or by their deaths, ſuch eſtates do deſcend to "their heirs, whereby the clerk of the crown of "the ſaid court is rendered incapable to diſcern "where ſuch intereſt lies, until the perſon or per-"ſons, to whom ſuch eſtates are conveyed, deviſed "or deſcended, ſhall come into the ſaid court, "and make entry of ſuch their claim as afore-"ſaid." The entry of which claim is rightly looked upon as complete notice to thoſe, whom it concerns.

In further ſupport of my opinion, that the entering up or recording incumbrances, (ſuch as judgments for inſtance) ought to be looked upon as opening a repoſitory of intelligence, to which every perſon concerned might, and therefore ought, at his own peril to reſort, we muſt reflect, that parliament paſſed an act (*a*) for *the better diſcovery of judgments*, &c. in the different courts of record, twice from year to year by way of experiment, which they afterwards (*b*) made perpetual. Now if a purchaſer, to be affected by a judgment, muſt have expreſs notice of it, and the record be not ſuch expreſs notice, what ſenſe or meaning can be given to the preamble of this act? "Whereas "great miſchiefs and damages happen and come, "as well to perſons in their lifetimes, but more "often to their heirs, executors and adminiſtra-

(*a*) 4 & 5 Will. and Mary, c. 20; and 6 & 7 Will. and Mary, c. 14.
(*b*) 7 & 8 Will. 3. c. 36.

" tors, and also to purchasers and mortgagees, by " judgments entered upon record in their Maje- " sties courts at Westminster, against the persons " defendants, by reason of the difficulty there is in " finding out such judgments." Now there can be no difficulty in finding out that, of which you have expreſs notice; for *giving notice* is nothing more nor leſs, than informing a perſon, in what court, at what time, for what ſum, and in whoſe name the judgment is entered up. And therefore becauſe parliament judged very obviouſly and wiſely, that if the entries were regularly and openly kept of theſe incumbrances, it would be (as it ought to be) the fault of a purchaſer, if he did not look into the dogget himſelf: and therefore I conceive, notwithſtanding any determination before or ſince this act, that a purchaſer is not affected by a judgment recorded, without expreſs notice thereof; yet that by this act, the doggeting of the judgment is ſufficient notice thereof to a purchaſer. At leaſt I cannot otherwiſe underſtand the following clauſe: " And be it further enacted, by the authority afore- " ſaid, that no judgment not doggeted and en- " tered in the books as aforeſaid, ſhall affect any " lands or tenements as to purchaſers or mortga- " gees, or have any preference againſt heirs, exe- " cutors or adminiſtrators, in their adminiſtration " of their anceſtors, teſtators or inteſtates eſtates." Does not the regular doggeting of judgments (the want of which renders them ineffectual againſt purchaſers and mortgagees) ſuppoſe that they are to be ſearched for; and if they are not (when regularly doggeted) notice to purchaſers and mortgagees, why are they to be ſearched for, and how can they affect them?

According to the ſenſe and ſpirit, in which I underſtand both the language of theſe ſtatutes and of our books, it is no ſmall ſatisfaction to find my opinion

opinion expreſsly warranted by the authority of Lord Hardwicke, in the caſe of *Hine* and *Dodd*, which was determined on the 13th March 1741 (*a*), in which a judgment creditor, whoſe judgment was regiſtered in Middleſex on 12th June 1735, brought a bill to be let in upon an eſtate preferably to a mortgagee, whoſe mortgage had been regiſtered on the ſecond of the ſaid month of June, upon a ſuggeſtion, that the mortgagee had notice of the judgment, before the mortgage was executed, although it was regiſtered ten days before the regiſtry of the judgment. Much of this caſe turned upon the nature of the notice given to the mortgagee of the prior judgment, which is irrelevant to the ſubject under our preſent conſideration; but as to what immediately relates to it, nothing in my opinion can be more peremptorily deciſive, than the words of Lord Hardwicke, viz. "The "regiſter act, the 7th of Ann. c. 20. *is notice to the* "*parties, and a notice to every body:* and the rea- "ſon of this ſtatute was to prevent parole proofs "of notice, or not notice." And he is further reported to have ſaid in this cauſe, that if it were not ſo, this ſtatute would be mere waſte paper. This very clear and conſiſtent doctrine of Lord Hardwicke ſeems not to have been attended to by any modern writer upon this ſubject; for they all unexceptionably take up the doctrine delivered ſome years before that time by Sir Joſeph Jekyl, at the Rolls, on the 16th of February 1737, in the caſe of *Wrightſon* and al. v. *Hudſon* and al. (*b*); in which "it was reſolved, that theſe ſtatutes avoid "only prior charges not regiſtered, but did not "give ſubſequent conveyances any further force "againſt prior ones regiſtered, than they had be-

(*a*) 2 Atk. 275.
(*b*) 2 Eq. Ca. Abr. 609.

" fore: that to have affected Mr. Wrightſon, Hud-
" ſon ought to have given him notice, when he
" advanced his money; and though Wrightſon
" might have ſearched the regiſter, yet he was not
" bound to do it." I need make no comment upon theſe two deciſions: I will only repeat, that in the year 1737, Sir Joſeph Jekyl ſaid, that a man was not bound to ſearch the regiſter; and that Lord Hardwicke ſaid, in 1741, that *the regiſter was a notice to the parties, and a notice to every body.* What more contradictory than theſe two poſitions? For that which a man is not bound to look to, cannot be notice; and that which is notice, a man is bound to look to, as is ſelf-evident.

In this, as in ſome other inſtances, where I have taken the liberty to expreſs my own perſonal opinion upon points of law and equity, I have done it with a view, that the legiſlature may be induced by one efficient act to reduce the ſtatutes, which relate to the ſame ſubject, to conſiſtency both of ſpirit and letter, and the future deciſions of the courts of law and equity to plain rules and fixed principles.

I do not unexceptionally accede to the old obſervation, that Engliſhmen ſeldom make any good laws, till ſome common calamity cauſes them: but I flatter myſelf, that in this inſtance they will be ſenſible of the preſent inconveniences; and, foreſeeing much future good, will anticipate the remedy to the further evil conſequences of the diſeaſe, and thus contradict, what Dr. Swift obſerved, *that Engliſhmen can feel but not ſee.* And I think it no impertinent queſtion to propoſe; Who does not ſee, that the obvious purpoſe of recording a deed is, that thoſe, whom it concerns may take notice of it?

But it muſt be remembered, that the regiſtering of a deed is not recording it, as the *inrolment* of a deed a deed is; nor is a deed abſolutely null for want of being regiſtered: whereas, according to the ſyſtem, which I have undertaken to ſuggeſt and recommend, no deed nor will affecting land will be valid, unleſs it ſhall be inrolled within a limited time; and upon this ground, the argument for a deéd inrolled being notice to all mankind, will acquire infinitely more ſtrength, and will fall directly under the reaſon and doctrine of Lord Hardwicke, in *Hine* and *Dodd*. The principle of this doctrine appears clearly to be, that the regiſtering acts are meant to operate upon all ſubſequent incumbrancers, who ſhall not have received actual notice of a prior incumbrance, by affording them the means of acquiring that knowledge, which will be equivalent to actual notice. So Lord Hardwicke (*a*) decreed, that "if a deed "reſpecting lands in any of the regiſtering coun-"ties be not regiſtered, and afterwards the ſame "lands are ſold or mortgaged by a deed properly "regiſtered, if the perſon claiming under the ſe-"cond deed has notice of the firſt deed, the perſon "claiming under the firſt deed, though it be not "regiſtered, ſhall be preferred to him." Such a deciſion could not have been made, if the regiſtery were neceſſary to the validity of the deed, as is ſelf evident (*b*)." And a ſubſequent mortgagee having notice of a prior mortgage not regiſtered, will not gain a priority by regiſtering, "becauſe ſuch conduct is conſidered in equity as "fraudulent, and the party hath that notice, which "the act of parliament intended he ſhould have." What more clear, than that the act intended that the regiſtering of a deed ſhould operate as notice,

(*a*) Le Neve v. Le Neve, 1 Vez. 64.

(*b*) Cowper's Rep. 712 and Powell upon the Law of Mortgage, 287.

which

which would be abſurd in the extreme, if a man ſearched the regiſtery at his own peril: for it is evidently more advantageous to a purchaſer or mortgagee to complete his purchaſe or mortgage *without* notice, than *with* notice of a prior incumbrance.

In my preſent purſuit, it is not only my duty to ſtate, what the law of *notice* now is, but more eſpecially what under the propoſed act of parliament it ought to be. And I am happy in being able to confirm the doctrine of Lord Hardwicke, in *Hine* and *Dodd*, by the more minute and expreſs opinion of the famed D'Agueſſeau, chancellor of France. (*a*) By laws of that kingdom, as ancient as the ſixteenth century, particularly an ordonnance of Henry the Second, of the year 1553, it was ordered that all wills and deeds, containing ſubſtitutions of eſtates, ſhould be regiſtered within a particular period of time. If they were not regiſtered within that time, the courts ſeem to have doubted whether they were binding even on the parties, in whoſe favour the ſubſtitutions were made; but it was always ſettled, that the ſubſtitutions were of no force againſt creditors or purchaſers. Several points of the laws reſpecting ſubſtitutions being unſettled, and the laws reſpecting them being different in different parts of the kingdom, they were all reduced into one law by the celebrated ordonnance of Auguſt 1747. That ordonnance was framed by the chancellor D'Agueſſeau, after taking the ſentiments of every parliament in the kingdom upon forty-five different queſtions propoſed to them upon the ſubject. The thirty-ninth queſtion is, "Whether a creditor or "purchaſer, having notice of the ſubſtitution be-"fore his contract or purchaſe, is to be admitted

(*a*) Harg. and Butler's Co. Lit. 291.

"to

"to plead the want of regiſtration?" All the parliaments, except the parliament of Flanders, agreed that he was; that to admit the contrary doctrine would make it always open to argument, whether he had or had not notice of the ſubſtitution; and this would lead to endleſs uncertainty, confuſion, and perjury; and that it was much better, that the right of the ſubject ſhould depend upon certain and fixed principles of law, than upon rules and conſtructions of equity, which muſt be arbitrary, and conſequently uncertain. The ordonnance of Auguſt 1747 was framed accordingly. Thoſe, who have commented upon that ordonnance, lay it down as a fixed and undeniable principle, that nothing, not even the moſt actual and direct notice, countervails the want of regiſtration; ſo that if a perſon is a witneſs, or even a party to the deed of ſubſtitution, ſtill if it is not regiſtered he may ſafely purchaſe the property ſubſtituted, or lend money upon a mortgage of it. See queſtions concernant les Subſtitutions, Thoulouſe 1770, and Commentaire de l'Ordonnance de Louis XV. Sur les Subſtitutions, par Mr. Furgole, a Paris, 1767.

### *Practical Applications.*

Let us now, abſtractedly from any prejudice of education, habit or profeſſion, argue upon this matter in the dictates of plain common ſenſe. A man wiſhes to purchaſe or place out a ſum of money upon mortgage, or to buy a rent-charge or annuity, iſſuing out of land. A title is propoſed to him; he ſubmits it to his law agent, who probably carries it to a conveyancing council; he peruſes and approves of the title, as ſubmitted to him in the abſtract; but directs the ſollicitor, who brought him the abſtract, to examine if the *grant* or *fine* or *recovery*, or *act of parliament*, upon which the

the title may hinge, be faithfully abſtracted from the record. This is the duty of a conveyancer; for he can only judge of what he ſees, and direct what may be effected. The client with the approbation of council confides in the ſecurity, and preſumes himſelf out of the reach of any impoſition in the tranſaction, and will naturally conclude, not only, that every ſtep has been taken, that can ſecure the title, but that no means nor power are left with the vendor or mortgagor or grantor of the annuity or rent-charge of overreaching or deceiving him in the title. And will he not moreover naturally conclude, if there be any repoſitory of information to reſort to concerning a man's title to land, that if it be not a ſource of ſatisfactory and concluſive intelligence, it muſt lead to deceit and error, by inſuring doubt and uncertainty?

What then is the fact? A vendor or mortgagor may notwithſtanding all, that has appeared to counſel upon the face of the abſtract, and all the intelligence and information, which the moſt diligent and attentive ſollicitor can by poſſibility acquire, have previouſly ſold, mortgaged, charged, or ſettled the whole or any parts of the land in queſtion, without an obligation of rendering notorious any one act, by which he may have made ſuch ſale, mortgage, charge or ſettlement. Whence then ariſes the neceſſity, or even expediency, of making public and notorious ſome acts, which affect the title of lands, whilſt the owner is empowered to ſuppreſs many others, by which he can equally affect them? He cannot cut off the expectant rights of a child or a remainder-man in an entailed eſtate, but by matter of notoriety and record: and is there not as much or more reaſon, why that act ſhould be public and notorious, by which a tenant in fee-ſimple counteracts and defeats the known, ſettled and certain courſe of the

law,

law, which would have caſt the inheritance upon the heir at law, if he had not counteracted and defeated its effects; and this he has it in his power to do by a private deed in his lifetime, or by will after his deceaſe; neither of which needs to be rendered public or notorious. He may by a private deed charge all his lands with a debt; but by confeſſing a judgment, which equally charges them, it muſt be by matter of record and notoriety.

I may be blamed and cenſured by ſome, for divulging the *arcana* of the profeſſion, and uttering truths, which may be thought to diſturb the peace and quiet of many, whoſe money is now placed out upon landed ſecurities; but I can neither invent nor conceive a ſtronger reaſon, why the law ſhould be altered, than becauſe the knowledge of it diſturbs the peace and endangers the ſecurity of individuals. It is then a truth no leſs certain than extraordinary, that in paſſing many titles of land, it is abſolutely neceſſary, that very great reliance and eſſential confidence ſhould be placed in the perſonal honour and integrity of individuals, againſt whoſe deceit, fraud and impoſition, ſhould they not be honeſt and honourable, there are abſolutely no means of providing. To prove this, I will ſtate a caſe that has very lately happened, which as to many points applies ſtrictly to my argument. I have met with ſeveral other caſes within my own knowledge, which turn upon the ſame point. But ſhould even the caſe I put, be merely ſuppoſitious, from the probability of its frequently happening, it would equally enforce my arguments.

## *The Cases of Rickman against Morgan (a), and Pearson against Morgan (b).*

Mr. James Butler of Suffex was entitled, under his father's marriage-fettlement, to an eftate charged with £. 8000 for one younger child of the marriage; which fettlement contained a provifo, that if the father fhould give to any of his daughters or younger fons any money or lands, for or in advancement in marriage, or otherwife, the value thereof fhould be deducted from the portion, unlefs he fhould by writing declare to the contrary. The father gave the refidue of his perfonal eftate to his only younger child Mr. John Butler, and made other advancements to him during his life. The father being dead, Mr. James Butler fuffered a common recovery, by which he obtained a fee-fimple in the lands. In 1773, Mr. John Butler applied to Mr. Pearfon to lend him £. 3000 on the fecurity of the £. 8000 portion, for which he affigned £. 5000, part of the faid £. 8000, as a fecurity. Mr. James Butler, who from the time of his fuffering the common recovery, held the fee-fimple of the eftate to his death, paid the intereft of the £. 8000. Mr. Pearfon, before he lent the money, applied by his follicitor, Mr. Hull, to Mr. James Butler, and defired to be informed by him, whether the £. 8000 was a fubfifting charge on the eftate; when Mr. James Butler declared that it was, and that he might fafely advance his money on the fecurity. Mr. James Butler had poffeffion of the fettlement, and knew of the advancements of the father to his brother; but not fuppofing the portion

(a) Brown's Reports, Vol. I. p. 63.

(b) D° Cafes argued and determined in 28th of his prefent Majefty, p. 334.

tion

tion affected by them nor by the gift of the residue, did not reveal the same to Mr. Pearson's sollicitor. Upon the death of Mr. James Butler some time after, his estates descended upon his two daughters. The husband of one of them (Mr. Bennet) in 1774 had also advanced £. 2978 to Mr. John Butler, upon the security of the £. 8000 portion, (subject to the first £. 3000 advanced by Mr. Pearson). Upon the 24th of last June, Mr. Justice Buller, sitting for Lord Chancellor, said, "he strongly inclined to think "it a satisfaction;" and the Lord Chancellor himself, on the 27th of last November, decreed the gift of the residue to be a satisfaction for the portion secured by the marriage-settlement. But as to the £. 3000 lent by Mr. Pearson, the Court held, that Mr. James Butler's declaration to the lender's sollicitor bound both him and his lands; and that sum was therefore directed to be raised and paid to Mr. Pearson. But no relief hath been given to Mr. Bennet for the money he advanced.

If Mr. James Butler had remained tenant in tail of the estates charged with £. 8000, and he had died insolvent as to his personality, I know not what redress Mr. Pearson would have had; but he had acquired the fee simple, and it was bound in equity by his verbal undertaking. It is not possible to adduce a stronger instance than this case, to prove the truth of what I have advanced concerning the necessity there often is of making personal confidence the ground of opinion in the approbation of a landed security for money. The words of the Court, in delivering the decree in this cause, are: "The enquiry was a very proper one "on the part of the plaintiff (viz. Pearson) and "completely repels the imputation of negligence "in his agent; and the enquiry was properly made "of the party immediately interested. James at "the

" the time of the enquiry, had the equitable inte- " rest in the estate, and upon the application, as- " sured the plaintiff, that he might safely lend his " money: the enquiry was the most material the " plaintiff could make." It appears from the case, that Mr. Hull was also concerned for Mr. Bennet, and it is to be presumed, that having done (by the confession of the Court) whatever he could do, to acquire the knowledge and information which was requisite for his client to know about the charge and term, upon the security of which Mr. Pearson lent his money, he could retain no doubt about recommending it to his other client Mr. Bennet, who lent £. 2978 upon the same security, the repayment of which has not as yet been decreed. The material point of law in this case, was the decision, after several hearings, that the residue of a personal estate is to be taken as a satisfaction for a portion. As this point had not before been decided, it could not be imputed to the negligence nor ignorance of the agent or his conveyancer, (who was very eminent in the profession, and is since dead) that they did not object against the security upon this ground. But as to my argument, it would have been the same, if all the advancements had been made by the father in his lifetime. Here was no attempt at fraud in either of the Messrs. Butler; but in this supposition, there were no sure means of coming at the knowledge of the prior advancements. The law required no sort of notoriety to attend the fact: both sons denied it; the conveyancer was not to suppose, what was not stated to him; the agent could not acquire the information, to submit it to the conveyancer: and thus, without any blame imputable to the agent; without any reflection upon the conveyancer, Mr. Pearson but for the personal and accidental undertaking of Mr. James

Butler, would have been) and Mr. Bennet actually is expoſed to the loſs of a large ſum of money under all the ſanction, protection and ſecurity, which the law, as it now ſtands, affords him for his property. I go ſtill farther; for, ſuppoſing a conveyancer ſhould ſtate the ſtrongeſt doubts, whether the whole or part of the fortune had been advanced or raiſed, yet are there no poſſible means of acquiring this knowledge for certain, againſt the determination of the two ſons to ſuppreſs the facts.

The ancient law and policy of our anceſtors could not, conſiſtently with that notoriety, which, as I have ſo often ſaid, they thought neceſſary to attend every act of alienation or affection of landed property, admit into conveyances of land, all thoſe modern *reſtraining* and *enabling* powers, the creation, execution and effects of which, have conſtituted a very conſiderable branch of equity. But of the doctrine of powers, it is not my purpoſe to ſay any more, than that from their very nature, the want of notoriety in the creation, as well as execution of them, muſt ever leave to purchaſers and mortgagees much perſonal confidence to rely upon for the ſecurity of their titles. And ſince a great part of family ſettlements at preſent turns upon theſe very powers, under which the portions for the younger children of families are often provided and ſecured, it becomes very eſſential and important to the community, that theſe titles ſhould be clear and certain; for when ſuch portions are raiſed and paid to younger children, it rarely happens, that the owners of the lands, which are charged with them, are capable of paying off the money, and it is generally done by others, who advance it upon the ſecurity or under the deed creating the powers. And if there can poſſibly exiſt a confederacy between father and ſon, or the younger children themſelves and their truſtees, or even if impoſition, treachery or deceit, may be ſuppoſed to exiſt in any one of them; by what means can the moſt attentive attorney, the moſt cautious conveyancer, and the moſt wary lender, prevent, counteract, or hinder the fraud? We have ſeen the effects of involuntary error in the judgment of Meſſrs. Butler. How neceſſary then it is to eſtabliſh an unerring ſource of notoriety and information, which every purchaſer, lender or mortgagee may reſort to with confidence and certainty? For it is evident, that where one part of a title muſt be made public and notorious, and the other part of it requires no ſuch notoriety, there ever will exiſt more doubt and uncertainty about the ſuppreſſed part of the title, than if none of it had been made public. What has been ſaid, will I hope be concluſive, that no charge nor diſcharge of land ought to be effected, but by a deed or act of public notoriety.

*More circumſtantial Proofs.*

The more we reflect upon this ſubject, the more circumſtances ſhall we find, that render the notoriety I have been ſpeaking of, more neceſſary at preſent, than at any paſt period of time. The firſt of theſe is the more general ſubdiviſion and equal partition of landed property: by which means, titles are multiplied and become more complex by derivation, and therefore leſs certain, becauſe leſs notorious, for want of title deeds; which, when eſtates are tranferred in parcels, or otherwiſe partially affected, cannot be delivered over to each purchaſer or incumbrancer, as if the whole eſtate, to which the deeds are the muniments, had been ſold or affected together. And I know no reaſon, which more emphatically proves the expediency of my propoſal, than the doctrine and preſent law concerning the delivery, poſſeſſion and cuſtody, of title deeds.

### *Of Title Deeds.*

The caſes, which have been determined, relative to the delivery, poſſeſſion and cuſtody, of title deeds and notice to purchaſers and incumbrancers, have very frequently ariſen from matters in regiſtering counties. But whatever relates to the regiſtering acts, ſhall be reſerved for future conſideration.

I do not find that the delivery, actual poſſeſſion or cuſtody of the title deeds, is eſſential to the validity of a purchaſe or mortgage; for a man ſeiſed in fee-ſimple of ten thouſand acres of land may validly mortgage or ſell it out in five hundred parcels, and yet it will be impoſſible to deliver title deeds to each mortgagee and purchaſer. And if the delivery of the title deeds were eſſential to the validity of a mortgage or purchaſe, yet in many caſes, it would be of no avail, eſpecially ſince it has been the general practice to make two and ſometimes more original parts of one and the ſame deed, (and without any thing appearing upon the face or back of ſuch deeds, to ſhew how many parts of them were executed). A man having collected for ſixty years back duplicates of all his title deeds, might at different times make out ſuch a title, as would and muſt, in the nature of buſineſs, be approved of by counſel, and ſell and mortgage the land to A. which he had previouſly ſold or mortgaged to B. without a poſſibility of the preconveyance being diſcovered by the moſt diligent attorney, or ſcrupulous and intelligent conveyancer.

## *A supposed Case.*

I will ſuppoſe two common recoveries ſuffered, and two marriage ſettlements made ſucceſſively of the manor of Dale; and theſe to run back into the laſt century. The reverſion in fee, under the ſecond ſettlement, veſts in the heir at law of the ſettler. He is in poſſeſſion of the land, and of two ſets of theſe ſettlements, which are the title deeds, and prove, to the ſatisfaction of the conveyancer, the right and title of the reverſioner's heir at law. If theſe original ſettlements are given up to a purchaſer, and it is known from examination, or from official extracts, that the recoveries have been well ſuffered, the ſettlements themſelves being the deeds to make the tenants to the *præcipe*, (or what by nonprofeſſional perſons are called the recovery deeds); I ſay that a conveyancer is *functus officio*, by approving of the title, and recommending the purchaſe or mortgage: and even ſhould he ſtate in his opinion the poſſibility of a preconveyance or ſale or mortgage to another perſon, I know of no means whatever, by which ſuch ſuggeſtion of doubt could be cleared away to his monied client, nor of any remedy that his client would have againſt the land or the prior purchaſer or mortgagee. For I think, that it will be readily allowed, that the perſonal aſſeverations, pledges and covenants of a perſon ſo void of good faith as to attempt ſuch a fraud, will afford but ſlight relief to this ſecond purchaſer or mortgagee. Such a caſe could not by poſſibility happen, if every deed was null without inrolment, and the inrolment was full notice to a purchaſer or mortgagee.

*A real*

### *A real Caſe anonymous.*

A perſon, in a large trading maritime town, had taken a long building leaſe of an extenſive piece of ground: he mortgaged parts of it to two perſons ſucceſſively, and delivered copies of his title deeds to the mortgagees, alledging, that he could not deliver up the original title deeds, as they affected other lands beſides thoſe, that were mortgaged, which he had in contemplation to aſſign and underlet in different parcels: at length, after he had twice mortgaged the ſame parcels of ground, without giving any notice of the firſt mortgages, he procures a third perſon to advance him a ſum of money upon them, larger than either of the two firſt mortgages; and to this third mortgagee he delivers his title deeds. The queſtion is, to whoſe debt ſhall the land be firſt liable? For it will barely anſwer one of the ſums advanced upon it. I need not ſay, that the perſonal reſponſibility of this iniquitous mortgagor is of little avail. The caſe is intended to be brought into court. How neceſſary for the prevention of ſuch practices, is a repoſitory of infallible certitude, by which a lender may know the ſecurity, upon which he advances his money?

### *Of the Regiſtry of Deeds and Wills by Act of Parliament.*

I cannot introduce this ſubject more properly, than by repeating the preamble of the 2d and 3d of Queen Ann, which was the precedent and ſample of the other regiſtering acts. And what this act recites of the weſt-riding of the county of York will appear at preſent more applicable to the nation at large, on account of the extended ſtate of its commerce, than it was at that time applicable to the weſt-riding of the county of York. "Whereas the weſt-riding of the county of "York is the principal place in the north for "the cloath manufactory, and moſt of the traders "therein are freeholders, and have frequent oc-"caſions to borrow money upon their eſtates, for "managing their ſaid trade, but for want of a "regiſter, find it difficult to give ſecurity to the "ſatisfaction of the money-lenders, (although the "ſecurity they offer be really good); by means "whereof the ſaid trade is very much obſtructed, "and many families ruined." Such was the ſenſe of the legiſlature, reſpecting a very populous and trading diſtrict; and ſuch, I am confident, to the conſiderate part of the nation, will it be for the country at large, in order to enable vendors and mortgagors to make ſuch clear and ſatisfactory titles, as will induce monied men to inveſt their money in real ſecurities. One and the ſame principle actuated them in that and the other three regiſtering acts, and us in our preſent attempt. Let us conſider the means they have adopted, to carry that principle into practice.

There is not a doubt, but that theſe regiſtries were planned, formed and eſtabliſhed, for the mutual benefit and conveniency of lenders and borrowers of money on land ſecurity. The preamble of an act is called by Lord Coke, the key to open the meaning and intent of the ſtatute; and by the preamble to the firſt regiſtering act of Queen Ann, which has been quoted, it evidently appears, that the evil intended to be remedied by the ſtatute was the want of notoriety in the titles of land owners, from which the inveſting of money in purchaſes and on mortgages was obſtructed and rendered difficult. Let us then ſee, what remedy, and in what manner, the act has provided againſt this evil.

It enacts, that (*a*) " a memorial of all deeds " and conveyances, which from and after the nine " and twentieth day of September in the year of " our Lord one thouſand ſeven hundred and four, " ſhall be made and executed, and of all wills " and deviſes in writing made or to be made and " publiſhed, where the deviſor or teſtator ſhall die " after the ſaid nine and twentieth day of Sep- " tember, of or concerning, and whereby any ho- " nors, manors, lands, tenements or hereditaments, " in the ſaid weſt-riding, may be any way af- " fected in law or equity, may, at the election of " the party or parties concerned, be regiſtered in " ſuch a manner, as is hereinafter directed; and " that every deed or conveyance that ſhall, at any " time after any memorial is ſo regiſtered, be made " and executed of the honors, manors, lands, te- " nements or hereditaments, or any part thereof, " comprized or contained in any ſuch memorial, " ſhall be adjudged fraudulent and void againſt " any ſubſequent purchaſer or mortgagee for va- " luable conſideration, unleſs ſuch memorial there- " of ſhall be regiſtered, as by this act is directed, " before the regiſtering of the memorial of the " deed or conveyance, under which ſuch ſubſe- " quent purchaſer or mortgagee ſhall claim; and " that every deviſe by will of the honors, manors, " lands, tenements or hereditaments, or any part " thereof mentioned or contained in any memo- " rial ſo regiſtered as aforeſaid, that ſhall be " made and publiſhed after the regiſtering of ſuch " memorial, ſhall be adjudged fraudulent, and void " againſt any ſubſequent purchaſer or mortgagee " for valuable conſideration, unleſs a memorial of " ſuch will be regiſtered in ſuch manner as is here- " inafter directed."

(*a*) 2 & 3 Ann, c. 4.

And it enacts, that " all and every memorials " so to be entered or registered, shall be put into " writing, in vellum or parchment, and directed " to the register of the said office; and in case of " deeds and conveyances, shall be under the hand " and seal of some or one of the grantors, or some " or one of the grantees, his or their guardians " or trustees, attested by two witnesses, one where- " of to be one of the witnesses to the execution " of such deed or conveyance; which witness shall, " upon his oath before the said register or his de- " puty, prove the signing and sealing of the said " memorial, and the execution of the deed or " conveyance mentioned in such memorial; and " in case of wills, the memorials shall be under " the hand and seals of some or one of the devi- " sees, his or their guardians or trustees, attested " by two witnesses, one whereof shall, upon his " oath before the said register or his deputy, prove " the signing and sealing of such memorial; which " respective oaths, the said register or his deputy, " is hereby impowered to administer."

And it further enacts, that " every memorial " of any deed, conveyance or will, shall contain " the day of the month, and the year, when such " deed, conveyance or will, bears date, and the " names and additions of all the parties to such " deed or conveyance, and of the devisor, or testa- " trix to such will, and of all the witnesses to such " deed, conveyance or will, and the places of their " abode, and shall express or mention the honors, " manors, lands, tenements and hereditaments, " contained in such deed, conveyance or will, and " the names of all the parishes, townships, ham- " lets, precincts or extraparochial places, within " the said west-riding, where any such honors, " manors, lands, tenements or hereditaments, are " lying or being, that are given, granted, convey-

" ed,

" ed, devised, or any way affected or charged by " any such deed, conveyance or will, in such man- " ner, as the same are expressed or mentioned in " such deed, conveyance or will, or to the same " effect; and that every such deed, conveyance " and will, or probate of the same, of which such " memorial is so to be registered, as aforesaid, " shall be produced to the said register or his de- " puty, at the time of entering such memorial, " who shall indorse a certificate on every such deed, " conveyance and will, or probate thereof, and " therein mention the certain day, hour and time, " on which such memorial is so entered and re- " gistered, expressing also in what book, page and " number, the same is entered; and that the said " register, or his deputy, shall sign the said certi- " ficate when so indorsed; which certificates shall " be taken and allowed as evidence of such re- " spective registries in all courts of record what- " soever; and that every page of such register- " books, and every memorial, which shall be en- " tered therein, shall be numbered, and the day " of the month, and the year, and hour, or time " of the day, when every memorial is registered, " shall be entered in the margins of the said re- " gister books, and of the said memorial; and that " every such register shall keep an alphabetical " calendar of all parishes, extraparochial places " and townships within the said west-riding, with " reference to the number of every memorial, that " concerns the honors, manors, lands, tenements, " or hereditaments, in every such parish, extrapa- " rochial place, or township respectively, and the " names of the parties mentioned in such memo- " rial; and that such register shall duly file every " such memorial in order of time, as the same " shall be brought to the said office, and enter or

" regifter the faid memorials in the fame order, " that they fhall refpectively come to hand."

There is an exception, that the act fhall not extend to copyhold eftates, or to any leafe not exceeding twenty-one years, where the actual poffeffion and occupation goes along with the leafe. It is obvious, why copyhold eftates are taken out of the ftatute; for their furrender in the manor court anfwers the notoriety of transfer, which was evidently intended to be introduced and eftablifhed throughout the weft-riding of the county of York by the regiftry.

The 2d and 3d of Ann, for eftablifhing a regiftry in the weft-riding of York, was the firft act relating to the regiftry that paffed; and although the framers of that act appear not to have been complete mafters of the fubject; yet it gave rife to the experiment, and turned people's thoughts more to the fubject, which, by the following regiftering acts, received fome additional light and improvement. Each of thefe acts moft pointedly tends to eftablifh the principles, grounds and reafons, upon which I am attempting to fhew the expediency, or rather the neceffity, of an univerfal inrolment. As much, as hath been quoted of the firft regiftering act, is repeatedly enacted by the other acts, which fucceffively eftablifhed the regiftry in the eaft-riding of the county of York, in the 6th of Queen Ann; in the county of Middlefex, in the 7th of Queen Ann; and in the north-riding of the county of York, in the 8th of George II.

The firft regiftering act paffed in 1703; and in 1706, it was found proper to pafs (*a*) " An act " *for inrolment of bargains and fales within the faid* " *weft riding of the county of York in the regifter* " *office, there lately provided, and for making the faid*

(*a*) 5 Ann, c. 18.

" *regifter*

" *register more effectual.*" The primary reaſon for paſſing this act is ſet forth in the preamble of it: " Whereas by an act of parliament made in the " 27th year of the reign of King Henry the 8th, " intituled, *For inrolments of bargains and ſales,* " it is enacted, That no manors, lands, tenements " or other hereditaments, ſhall paſs, alter or change " from one to another, whereby any eſtate of in- " heritance or freehold ſhall be made or take " effect in any perſon or perſons, or any uſe there- " of to be made, by reaſon only of any bargain and " ſale thereof, except the ſaid bargain and ſale be " made by writing indented and ſealed, and in- " rolled in one of the king's courts of record at " Weſtminſter, or elſe within the ſame county or " counties, where the ſame manors, lands or tene- " ments, ſo bargained and ſold lie or be, before " the cuſtos rotulorum, and two juſtices of the " peace, and the clerk of the peace of the ſame " county or counties, or two of them at the leaſt, " whereof the clerk of the peace to be one; which " act hath been found by experience to be of little " or no uſe within the weſt-riding of the county of " York, as to the inrolments of bargains and ſales " within the ſaid weſt-riding, for that the clerk of " the peace thereof for the time being, who hath " the keeping of the ſaid inrolments within the " ſaid weſt-riding, is not by the ſaid act enjoined " to give any ſecurity for the ſafe keeping, nor " under any penalty for the negligent keeping of " the ſaid inrolments, nor is there by the ſaid act " any certain place appointed for the keeping " thereof: And whereas by an act of parliament " made in the ſecond year of his preſent Majeſty's " reign, intituled, An act for the public regiſtering " of all deeds, conveyances and wills, that ſhall be " made of any honors, manors, lands, tenements " or hereditaments, within the weſt-riding of the

" county

" county of York, after the nine and twentieth day " of September 1704; a public office hath been " erected and eſtabliſhed at Wakefield, within the " ſaid weſt-riding, at the public charge thereof, " for regiſtering and ſafe keeping of memorials, " of all deeds, conveyances and wills, within the " ſaid riding, and a public regiſter hath been " choſen, who hath according to the directions of " the ſame act, given ſufficient ſecurity for the due " execution of the ſaid office." There is certainly much good ſenſe and reaſon in this; and it applies as ſtrongly to every part of the nation, as it does to the weſt-riding of the county of York: but beſides the inconveniency and miſchief which is here alledged, there is another very objectionable circumſtance, that attends the preſent law; it creates and leaves a doubt in thoſe, who have occaſion to ſearch for any ſuch deed; for after having perhaps ſearched in vain the four courts of record, for the inrolment of a deed; from the infrequency of inrolling deeds with the clerk of the peace, it frequently does not occur to them to extend their ſearch to the county, where the lands lie; and if thought of, every one knows the little ſatisfaction, that probably would attend a ſearch, where there is no regular depoſit of the records, where there is no reſponſibility upon the clerks to preſerve them, no obligation to keep them orderly and open to inſpection, and little practice of entering them upon the rolls. Theſe are reaſons, which ſpeak the expediency of abſtracts being entered in each reſpective county, of deeds, which affect lands lying in divers counties, or which are inrolled in any one of the courts of record, as it is provided for by the draſt of the bill ſubjoined to theſe ſheets.

The act very properly therefore gives to every bargain and ſale inrolled in the regiſter office, at Wakefield, the ſame force, as if it had been inrolled

rolled in a court of record, or before the cuſtos rotulorum, &c. according to the requiſition of the act of Henry VIII. and regiſtered according to the ſecond and third of Ann.

In the firſt regiſtering act, no mention was made of judgments, ſtatutes and recognizances, which affect lands; and yet they ought to be as notorious and public, as deeds and wills affecting lands, in order that the title of the land may be open and known to mortgagees, incumbrancers and purchaſers. It is therefore enacted, that " no judgment, " ſtatute or recognizance (other than ſuch as ſhall " be entered into in the name and upon the pro- " per account of her Majeſty, her heirs and ſuc- " ceſſors) which ſhall be obtained, or entered into, " after the ſaid four and twentieth day of June " in the ſaid year of our Lord one thouſand ſeven " hundred and ſeven, ſhall affect or bind any ma- " nors, lands, tenements or hereditaments, ſituate, " lying and being in the ſaid weſt-riding, but only " from the time that a memorial of ſuch judgment, " ſtatute or recognizance, ſhall be entered at the " ſaid regiſter-office, expreſſing and containing, in " caſe of ſuch judgment, the names of the plain- " tiffs, and the names and additions therein of the " defendants, the ſums thereby recovered, and the " time of the ſigning thereof, and in caſe of ſta- " tutes and recognizances, expreſſing and con- " taining the date of ſuch ſtatute or recognizance, " the names, and additions of the cognizors and " cognizees therein, and for what ſums, and before " whom the ſame were acknowledged; and that in " order to the making an entry of ſuch memorials " of judgments, ſtatutes, and recognizances as " aforeſaid, the party and parties deſiring the ſame, " ſhall produce to and leave with the ſaid regiſter, " or his deputy, to be filed in the ſaid public or " regiſter office, a memorial of ſuch judgment,

" ſtatute or recognizance, ſigned by the proper " officer, who ſhall ſign ſuch judgment, or his ſuc- " ceſſor in the ſame office, or by the proper officer, " in whoſe office ſuch ſtatute or recognizance ſhall " be inrolled, together with an affidavit ſworn be- " fore one of the judges at Weſtminſter, or a " maſter in Chancery, that ſuch memorial was duly " ſigned by the officer, whoſe name ſhall appear to " be thereunto ſet; which memorial ſuch reſpec- " tive officer is hereby required to give ſuch plain- " tiff or plaintiffs, cognizee or cognizees, or his, " her or their executors or adminiſtrators, or at- " torney, or any of them, he, ſhe or they, paying " for the ſame the ſum of one ſhilling and no " more."

And there is a proviſo in the act, that " if any " judgment, ſtatute, or recognizance, be regiſtered " in the ſaid regiſter-office, within thirty days, " after the acknowledgment or ſigning thereof, " all the lands that the defendant or cognizor " had at the time of ſuch acknowledgment or " ſigning, ſhall be bound thereby."

But as it was found neceſſary to enter and pub-liſh every charge and incumbrance upon the land; ſo was it reaſonable, whenever theſe charges or incumbrances were ſatisfied and paid off, that the diſcharge or exoneration of the land ſhould alſo be known, as its value and price thereby would vary much to a purchaſer or incumbran-cer: for it frequently happens, that land is affected and incumbered by a deed, and the money or debt is diſcharged, without the parties entering into any new deed or writing, and therefore the act enacts, that " in caſe of mortgages, that ſhall " be inrolled in the ſaid regiſter-office, purſuant " to this act, or whereof memorials have been or " ſhall be entered, purſuant to the ſaid act made " in the ſecond year of her preſent Majeſty's reign; " and

" and alſo in caſe of judgments, ſtatutes and re-
" cognizances, whereof memorials ſhall be entered
" in the ſaid regiſter-office, purſuant to this act;
" if at any time afterwards, a certificate ſhall be
" brought to the ſaid regiſter or his deputy, ſigned
" by the reſpective mortgagors and mortgagees
" in ſuch mortgage, plaintiffs and defendants in
" ſuch judgment, cognizor or cognizees in ſuch
" ſtatute or recognizance reſpectively, their reſpec-
" tive executors, adminiſtrators or aſſigns, and at-
" teſted by two witneſſes, whereby it ſhall appear,
" that all monies due upon ſuch mortgage, judg-
" ment, ſtatute or recognizance reſpectively, have
" been paid or ſatisfied in diſcharge thereof, which
" witneſſes ſhall upon their oath, before the ſaid
" regiſter or his deputy, (who are hereby reſpec-
" tively impowered to adminiſter ſuch oath) prove
" ſuch monies to be ſatisfied or paid accordingly,
" and that they ſaw ſuch certificate ſigned by the
" ſaid mortgagors and mortgagees, plaintiffs and
" defendants, cognizors and cognizees reſpectively,
" their reſpective executors, adminiſtrators or aſ-
" ſigns; that then, and in every ſuch caſe, the
" ſaid regiſter or his deputy, ſhall make entry in
" the margin of the ſaid regiſter books, againſt
" the inrolment of ſuch mortgage or regiſtry of
" the memorial thereof, and againſt the regiſtry
" of ſuch judgment, ſtatute or recognizance re-
" ſpectively, that ſuch mortgage, judgment, ſta-
" tute or recognizance reſpectively, was ſatisfied
" and diſcharged according to ſuch certificate, to
" which the ſame entry ſhall refer; and ſhall after
" file ſuch certificate to remain upon record in the
" ſaid regiſter-office."

There is one ſingularity in this act, that I cannot paſs over without ſome obſervation; it enacts, that " all copies of the inrolments thereof remain-
" ing on record in the ſaid regiſter-office, ſhall be

" allowed

"allowed in all courts, where ſuch bargains and "ſales, or copies, ſhall be produced to be as good "and ſufficient evidence, as any bargains and ſales "inrolled in any of the courts at Weſtminſter, and "the copies of the inrolments thereof." This clauſe, as well as the other amendments of the ſecond and third of Ann, is introduced into the ſixth of Ann, by which a regiſter office is eſtabliſhed in the eaſt-riding of the county of York; and yet within four years after that time, viz. in the tenth of Ann (*a*), the legiſlature found it neceſſary to paſs an expreſs law to make office copies of bargains and ſales inrolled under the ſtatute of Henry the Eighth, evidence. Such different acts upon the ſame ſubject, argue but little knowledge of the law, in the framers of the acts: for if the tenth of Ann were neceſſary to be paſſed, the copies of bargains and ſales were not evidence in any court; and then this clauſe of the fifth of Ann is abſolutely futile and abſurd; for it does not abſolutely make ſuch copies evidence, but it only makes them *as much evidence* as other copies, which were not evidence at all; and if copies of inrolments were evidence before the tenth of Ann, then is that ſtatute nugatory and redundant and miſchievous, by confining its effects to one ſort of inrolled deeds, when it ought to have extended them to all; for many ſorts of deeds beſides bargains and ſales, were inrolled by the common law, before the ſtatute of Henry VIII. as they ſtill may be.

The preamble of the ſeventh of Queen Ann, for eſtabliſhing a regiſtry in the county of Middleſex, which is one and the ſame in effect as in the three other regiſtering acts, ſpeaks ſuch forcible language in ſupport of an univerſal inrolment act, that I cannot paſs it by unnoticed (*a*). "Whereas by

(*a*) 10 Ann, c. 18.

(*b*) 7 Ann, c. 20.

"the

" the different and ſecret ways of conveying lands, " tenements, and hereditaments, ſuch, as are ill " diſpoſed, have it in their power to commit fraud, " and frequently do ſo, by means whereof ſeveral " perſons, who through many years induſtry in " their trades and employments, and by great fru- " gality, have been enabled to purchaſe lands, or " to lend monies on land ſecurity, have been un- " done in their purchaſes and mortgages, by prior " and ſecret conveyances, and fraudulent incum- " brances; and not only themſelves, but their " whole families thereby utterly ruined."

Who will ſeriouſly admit even the poſſibility of ſuch evils, and deny that a remedy ought to be applied to them? And who will heſitate to anſwer this obvious queſtion? When land is brought to market, ſhould there exiſt a poſſibility of its being clogged with hidden charges and ſecret incumbrances? Beſides the alterations or improvements already mentioned, introduced into the regiſtering acts by the ſixth of Ann (all of which are incorporated by that act into the firſt regiſtering act for the weſt-riding) there is one other, which is introduced by that act into all the three acts for the three ſeveral ridings for the county of York, but which never was introduced into that for the county of Middleſex; I do not in fact ſee that it hath any immediate connection with the regiſtry or inrolment, any more than altering a form of pleading, has with recording a verdict or judgment (*a*)." " And be it further enacted by the authority aforeſaid, that in all deeds of bargain and ſale here- " after inrolled, in purſuance of this act, whereby " any eſtate of inheritance in fee-ſimple is limited " to the bargainee and his heirs, the words Grant, " Bargain, and Sale, ſhall amount to, and be con-

(*a*) 6 Ann, c. 35. ſect. 30.

" ſtrued and adjudged in all courts of judicature " to be expreſs covenants to the bargainee, his " heirs and aſſigns, from the bargainor, for himſelf, " his heirs, executors and adminiſtrators, that the " bargainor, notwithſtanding any act done by him, " was at the time of the execution of ſuch deed " ſeiſed of the hereditaments and premiſſes thereby " granted, bargained and ſold, of an indefeaſible " eſtate in fee ſimple, free from all incumbrances " (rents and ſervices due to the lord of the fee " only excepted) and for quiet enjoyment thereof, " againſt the bargainor, his heirs and aſſigns, and " all claiming under him, and alſo for further " aſſurance thereof to be made by the bargainor, " his heirs and aſſigns, and all claiming under him, " unleſs the ſame ſhall be reſtrained and limited " by expreſs particular words contained in ſuch " deed; and that the bargainee, his heirs, executors, " adminiſtrators and aſſigns reſpectively, ſhall and " may in any action to be brought, aſſign a breach " or breaches thereupon, as they might do in caſe " ſuch covenants were expreſsly inſerted in ſuch " bargain and ſale."

This idea, I preſume, was borrowed from Sir Matthew Hale, who in the before-mentioned pamphlet (p. 37) ſays, " that to prevent the length of " covenants in deeds, there be thought of certain " words, that may carry in them the ſtrength of co- " venants or warranties; as for inſtance *(dedi,* or " *give)* to include a warranty and covenant againſt " all men, and alſo for further aſſurances; *(grant)* " to include a warranty and covenant againſt the " party and all claiming under him, and for fur- " ther aſſurances for ſeven years; *(deliver)* to in- " clude a warranty and covenant againſt the party " and his anceſtors and all claiming under them, " and for further aſſurances within ſeven years; " and divers inſtances of this kind might be con-

" tinued

" tinued by short words to include large sen-
" tences (*a*).

Certain it is, that the present mode of conveyancing is more formal and prolix, than is necessary to give effect to a deed. The nicety and extreme caution of some, the diffidence of others, and fear to omit any thing, that they can suppose will be binding in a deed, and perhaps the lucrative views of others, in extending conveyances with their wishes or love of gain, are the unjustifiable and unsatisfactory reasons for keeping on foot this formal prolixity in modern conveyances. But when we reflect, that every man is entitled to draw his own deeds and wills, and that he may use whatever words and terms he pleases to express his own meaning and intentions, and that each deed and will differs one from the other, it will not be found feasible to reduce conveyances, like certain writs and processes, to a fixed form of words, terms, and sentences. I shall say no more upon this subject, as it is not connected with the notoriety of deeds and muniments touching the title of lands: but if hereafter any innovation should be attempted to be introduced into the practice of conveyancing, it surely ought to be submitted in a full and comprehensive view to the legislature, that they may act therein as in their wisdom shall seem proper.

The last registering act, which is the eighth of Geo. the 2d, by which a register office was erected and established in the north-riding of the county of York, has no further improved upon any of the former registering acts, than by expressing a sense of the inefficient method of entering memorials in that inept, mutilated, and ineffectual manner prescribed by that act, as well as by the three other

(*a*) The word *grant* implies a general warranty; Croke Ja. 234. Hil. 7. Jac.

regiſtering acts: it gives licence to inrol deeds and wills at large, inſtead of regiſtering them in the manner before mentioned. It was rightly judged, that if a repoſitory was once eſtabliſhed for the memorials of deeds, it ought to be a complete conſervatory of men's titles to their eſtates. For this end, the purport of every deed ſhould be known, but by a memorial, the purport of no deed can be known.

(*a*) " And whereas deeds have been often de-
" ſtroyed by fire and other accidents, be it further
" enacted by the authority aforeſaid, that from
" and after the ſaid 29th day of September 1736,
" any perſon or perſons having or claiming title to
" any honors, manors, lands, tenements or he-
" reditaments, in the ſaid north-riding, may re-
" giſter at full length in the ſaid regiſter-office, all
" and every or any the deeds, writings, wills or
" conveyances, by or under which, ſuch title ſhall
" be claimed, and which ſhall be made and exe-
" cuted, or ſigned and publiſhed, and in the caſe
" of wills, where the deviſor or teſtatrix ſhall die
" after the ſaid 29th day of September in the year
" of our Lord 1736; and the ſaid regiſter or his
" deputy is hereby authorized to enter and inrol
" all ſuch deeds, writings, wills and conveyances,
" as ſhall be ſo brought to be regiſtered at full
" length, by ingroſſing them in parchment books;
" and the ſaid regiſter or his deputy ſhall, in the
" margin of every ſuch entry and inrolment, men-
" tion the time of ſuch entry and inrolment, and
" ſhall indorſe and ſign a certificate on ſuch deed,
" conveyance, or will, in manner, as is by this act
" directed, where a memorial is entered, and ſhall
" ſafely keep all and every the books, wherein ſuch
" entries and inrolments ſhall be made in the ſaid

(*a*) 8 Geo. 2. c. 6. ſect. 22.

" public office, there to remain upon record; and " all copies of ſuch entries and inrolments of ſuch " deeds, writings, wills and conveyances, ſo re- " giſtered at full length, and which copies ſhall be " ſigned by the ſaid regiſter or his deputy, and " atteſted by two or more witneſſes, ſhall be al- " lowed in all courts of record to be good and ſuf- " ficient evidence of ſuch deeds, writings, wills or " conveyances, ſo regiſtered and deſtroyed by fire " or other accident."

Can any thing be more unmanly and frivolous, than for the framers of ſo important an act of parliament, to acknowledge themſelves thus pub-licly ſenſible of a moſt material defect in the ſyſ-tem of regiſtering, and to point out the remedy, but leave it only optional, as if they were fearful of enjoining and compelling the means, which would be effectually remedial of the evil felt and complained of?

To the end a remedy may be complete, it muſt be commenſurate with the evil. Where then the evil conſiſts in the poſſibility of a land-owner's ſuppreſſing or falſifying his title, the remedy, to be commenſurate with the evil, ſhould take away this poſſibility; which nothing, that is not univer-ſally coercive, can effect. By the regiſtering acts, the entering the memorial of a deed is merely voluntary and optional; it neither gives nor takes away validity, it only ſecures in ſome caſes a pri-ority amongſt different incumbrancers.

### *The Conſequences of a Deed not regiſtered.*

To ſhew the conſequences and effects of theſe acts in a ſtronger light, we will ſuppoſe that a land-owner in the weſt-riding of the county of York, having an unincumbered landed property, ſettles it upon his family and dies. The deed, though not regiſtered, is to all intents and purpoſes valid againſt all mankind, except againſt a purchaſer or mortgagee; and I ſuppoſe none ſuch. His ſon takes under this ſettlement an eſtate in tail male: but finding it not regiſtered, keeps it in his own poſſeſſion; ſells the land, and dies without iſſue. His brother is, under the ſettlement, the next remainder man in tail male. Is it, or ſhould it be determined by law, that the neglect of the ſettler, which could not afterwards be rectified or ſupplied, ſhall have the effect of extinguiſhing the entail and barring the remainder man, who by the law ought only to be barred by the formality and notoriety of a fine or common recovery? If ſo, it would encourage and ſupport the groſſeſt fraud, deceit and impoſition. So much I ſuppoſe, if the deed creating the entail be not regiſtered.

### *The Conſequences of a Deed regiſtered.*

If I may be admitted freely to diſcuſs theſe acts of parliament, it muſt be allowed, that if a memorial of ſuch a deed be regiſtered according to the directions and in ſtrict compliance with every requiſition of the regiſtering acts, the confuſion, inconveniency and injuſtice, which might ariſe to all parties concerned in it, would be infinitely greater by the regiſtering of it, than if it had not been regiſtered.

My nonprofeſſional readers will excuſe my running into detail, in order the better to expoſe my reaſoning to a concluſive judgment. I will ſuppoſe an indenture of three parts made between the landowner of the firſt part, his intended wife of the ſecond part, and one or more truſtees of the third part; by which he ſettles his eſtate on himſelf and intended wife for life ſucceſſively, with a proviſion for younger children, with remainder to the

firſt

firſt and other ſons of the marriage in tail male, remainder to the firſt and other ſons of the ſettler by any other woman in tail male, remainder to the firſt and other daughter and daughters of the marriage, remainder to the ſettler's brother for life, remainder to his firſt and other ſon and ſons in tail male, remainder to the ſettler in fee; with powers to the two tenants for life of charging the lands with portions for their younger children, and of jointuring their wives, and with other powers of ſale, exchange, leaſing, and of revocation and new appointment by the ſettler. This deed being drawn, a memorial thereof is alſo prepared and executed at one and the ſame time with the deed. This memorial, according to the act, is under the hand and ſeal of the grantor or ſettler, atteſted by two witneſſes to the execution of the deed of ſettlement, and the execution thereof is proved by the oath of one of ſuch atteſting witneſſes. This memorial contains and ſets forth the date of the deed, and the exact deſcription of the parties to it, and the names and places of abode of the witneſſes to the execution of it by the party, who ſigns and ſeals the memorial, and ſuch of the parcels as lie in the diſtrict ſubject to the regiſtry. And when ſuch memorial ſhall have been entered, and a certificate indorſed upon the deed, mentioning the certain day, hour and time, on which ſuch memorial is ſo entered and regiſtered, and expreſſing alſo in what book, page and number, the ſame is entered, ſhall have been ſigned by the regiſter or his deputy, ſuch indorſed certificate ſhall be taken and allowed as evidence of the regiſtry in every court of record. Here then is a deed regiſtered in every particular, according to the requiſitions of the act of parliament. Let us attend to its effects.

As it is regiſtered according to the act, it is

good and valid againſt all mankind, even againſt purchaſers and mortgagees, to whom the memorial, as we have ſeen, is complete notice of any prior incumbrance created by that deed, at leaſt to every one, who has ſeen or is informed of the memorial. But a perſon of the moſt ordinary underſtanding, will naturally aſk, if a memorial ought to be, or in fact *can* be notice of what it does not diſcloſe nor mention. I ſuppoſe then an intended purchaſer of a part of this eſtate, upon an advertiſement for ſale, by the owner (who by the ſettlement is tenant for life only) ſearches the regiſter, and finds the above-ſtated memorial; and from whatever appears upon the face of it, he cannot tell whether it be the memorial of a marriage ſettlement, an aſſignment of mortgage, annuity deed, or, in ſhort, what is the nature, purport and effect of the deed. The tenant for life undertakes to ſell in fee-ſimple: the ſettlement is loſt, miſlaid, or depoſited perhaps with a mortgagee or lender of money, charged under the powers of the ſettlement itſelf. And in this latter caſe, the mortgagee may even in a court of equity refuſe to diſcover his title deeds, upon this ground, that a third perſon may find out a flaw in them. (*a*) It is aſſerted, that the deed in queſtion was merely a ſettlement of jointure upon the wife, who is dead, and of the land upon the iſſue male of the marriage, with the immediate reverſion in fee to the ſettler, who never had iſſue male, but has iſſue female, viz. three daughters: their proviſion he further aſſerts to be the fortune of their mother, veſted in the funds. The purchaſer completes his purchaſe of a part of theſe lands, pays his money, and enters. The father goes abroad, and dies out of the kingdom. One of the daughters pro-

(*a*) Senhouſe v. Earle, 2 Vez. 450. Parrat v. Bellard, 2 Ch. Ca. 73.—Ibid 135. 1 Vern. 27.

cures

cures the original ſettlement, and they enter upon the purchaſer, who certainly cannot maintain his title. For the deed, under which the daughters claim an eſtate tail, would have been a nullity againſt the purchaſer, if it had not been regiſtered; but having been regiſtered, and he having ſeen or been informed of the contents of the memorial, it is valid and concluſive againſt him, and he is preſumed in law to have been a purchaſer with full notice and knowledge of an eſtate tail prior to his own title: and this knowledge he is preſumed to have acquired through the medium of an act of law, intended undoubtedly to clear, manifeſt and eſtabliſh the right and title of the lands, in the purchaſe of which he has inveſted his money.

*The Miſchief of the regiſtering Acts.*

Innumerable caſes within the line of frequent occurrences might be ſtated, to ſhew the miſchievous conſequences and abſurdity of theſe acts. Why does the non-regiſtry of a deed or will render it null and void againſt a purchaſer or mortgagee? But becauſe, if not regiſtered, it is preſumed, that the eſtates and incumbrances created by them may be ſuppreſſed from his knowledge, and therefore that his title might afterwards be impeached and defeated by the prior incumbrancer, or taker under the valid deed. Why then ſhould the regiſtering of the deed prevent this effect? But becauſe the purchaſer or mortgagee is ſuppoſed to take his purchaſe or ſecurity with his eyes open, and with notice from the ſuppoſed notoriety of all prior charges by the memorial. And we have ſeen, that this ſuppoſed act of notoriety, does not even mention the conſideration of the deed; that is, whether it be a mortgage in fee or for years, whether it be for £. 500 or £. 10,000, whether there be be any limitations or powers of charging, ſelling, leaſing or other powers, or whether there are any ſhifting uſes, clauſes or proviſoes, contained in the deed, to affect the land.

It is uncontrovertibly obvious, that if a deed be intended to convey notice of a prior charge to a purchaſer or mortgagee, it muſt eſſentially give him certain and complete intelligence, to what extent the deed does actually affect the land: for in purchaſing or taking it in mortgage, he takes it liable and ſubject to all the limitations, truſts, powers, proviſoes, charges, conditions and covenants contained in the deed; of which, by the memorial, he is preſumed to have notice; but by which he could not poſſibly acquire any actual or real knowledge, intelligence, or information of them.

I have hitherto ſpoken of the knowledge, that is ſuppreſſed, or is not diſcloſed by the memorial; I muſt now ſpeak of that, which is acquired by it: and I ſpeak from experience. The mere knowledge of lands having been affected by a deed generally, is an endleſs ſource of unanſwerable difficulties, doubts and objections, in clearing a title: and every practitioner muſt often have experienced the truth of what Sir Matthew Hale foretold, long before any of the regiſtering acts were paſſed (*a*). "There muſt be inrolled at leaſt ſo much of "the deed or evidence, that concerns, firſt, parties, grantor and grantee; ſecondly, the things "granted; thirdly, the eſtate granted; fourthly, "all thoſe parts of the deed or evidence, that "have any influence upon the eſtate, as, rent reſerved, conditions, powers of revocation, of al- "teration, of leaſing, the truſts, &c. and thoſe

(*a*) The aforeſaid treatiſe of regiſtering deeds and wills, p.

" other things, which have an influence upon the " eſtate: and without all this done, and truly done, " the purchaſer or lender is as much in the dark as " before, and cheated under the credit of a public " office erected to prevent it."

The regiſtering acts, though well meant, and intended to produce the happieſt effects, were unfortunately framed and penned by perſons, who muſt have been groſsly ignorant of, or wholly inattentive to the firſt principles of conveyancing. For the rudeſt novice in that art ſhould be ſenſible, that no memorial or entry of a deed could benefit a purchaſer or mortgagee, which did not diſcloſe ſome knowledge of the title to the lands ſold or mortgaged; and that a general confuſed aſſurance, that ſomething had been done to affect the land, without any ſpecification of the fact, muſt enſure an infinity of doubt, ſuſpicion, perplexity and inconveniency, to every purchaſer and mortgagee.

*A Regiſtry ought to be a Conſervatory of Men's Title Deeds.*

One obvious and very important advantage of deeds being regiſtered and preſerved in a public repoſitory, ſhould be the perpetuation of men's titles to their eſtates, in caſe of the loſs or deſtruction of their original deeds. It certainly tends much to ſecure the title to an eſtate, when ſuch reſort may be had to a ſure ſource of information: elſe why the repoſitory of records in general, of fines and recoveries, of ſtatutes, of bargains and ſales, and the probate and preſervation of wills? In the earlieſt acts of parliament, which have been paſſed concerning the inrolment of titulary documents, &c. we perceive that the legiſlature entered into the true ſpirit and intent of ſuch repoſitories or conſervatories, that they might anſwer the double

double end of notoriety and perpetuation, and manifeſtation and defence of the owner's right and title to his lands (*a*). " It is ordained and eſta-
" bliſhed, that all the writs of covenants, &c. before
" that they be drawn out of the common bench by
" the chirographer, ſhall be inrolled in a roll, to
" be of record, for ever to remain in the ſafe cuſ-
" tody of the chief clerk of the common bench
" and his ſucceſſors, &c. to the intent that, if
" the notes in the cuſtody of the chirographer, or
" the fines be embeſiled, a man may have recourſe
" to the ſaid roll, to have execution thereof, as he
" ſhould have, if the fines were not embeſiled,
" &c."

There can be no reaſoning more juſt, than from parity of circumſtances. We ſee by the 3 & 4 Ed. 6. c. 4. *concerning the grants and gifts by patentees out of letters patent*, that where a " partial
" ſale, transfer, demiſe or ſettlement of an eſtate
" holden under a grant of the crown by letters pa-
" tent, is made by the patentee; any perſon claim-
" ing either immediately under the original grant,
" or by virtue of any ſuch ſale, transfer, demiſe
" or ſettlement, made by the patentee, may, by
" ſhewing forth an exemplification or *conſtat* of the
" inrolment, or even of ſo much thereof, as ſhall
" ſerve for the matter in variance, make and con-
" vey unto himſelf title by way of declaration,
" plaint, avowry, title, bar, or otherwiſe, againſt
" the crown and all other perſons; which exempli-
" fications (or copies) ſhall be of the ſame force
" and effect, as the letters patent."

In the preſent flouriſhing ſtate of commerce, and the neceſſarily conſequent circulation of property, eſtates are conſtantly undergoing ſome partial change or affection; and I ſee no reaſon, why

(*a*) 5 Hen. 4. c. 14.

a pura purchaser of what has formerly been crown land, should be enabled with more facility, than any other purchaser, to make a good title to the land he purchases. The reason therefore, which induced the legislature, in the year 1549, to make this provision for the security of some purchasers and claimants, is now, in the year 1789, submitted to the nation at large, for extending a similar provision to all purchasers and claimants indiscriminately: and this will be most efficiently done by requiring every deed and will affecting lands to be inrolled, and making office copies of such deeds evidence in all courts of justice.

It certainly is for the mutual advantage of buyer and seller, borrower and lender, that this conservatory should be useful. It cannot be so, if nothing be preserved in it, by which a title can be known, much less perpetuated. This is the end and intent of legal acts being recorded; and such is the effect of inrolling deeds; the nature of which we are now to consider.

## *Of the Inrolment of Deeds by common Law.*

If it be true, as the late Judge Blackstone said (*a*), that particular customs are a branch of the unwritten (or common) laws of England; but for reasons that have been now long forgotten, particular counties, cities, towns, manors and lordships, were very early indulged with the privilege of abiding by their own customs, in contradistinction to the nation at large; which privilege is confirmed to them by several acts of parliament: if it be an universal usage and custom in every copyhold estate throughout the nation, that every act of alienation is done with notoriety and pub-

(*a*) Bl. Com. sec. 3. p. 74.

licity within its own manor; that throughout the manor of Taunton, every deed affecting land be inrolled (*a*); if a deed inrolled within the city of London, acknowledged before the recorder and an alderman, and the woman examined, ſhall bind as a fine at law, by reaſon of the cuſtom anciently uſed; if the inrolment of deeds in corporate towns be confirmed by the ſtatute of uſes (*b*); may we not fairly infer, that it was the ancient uſage, cuſtom or law, to make every deed affecting land public and notorious, by inrolment or otherwiſe.

We read in the 34 and 35 H. 8. c. 22, "that "divers doubts, queſtions and ambiguities, had "ariſen, whether the recoveries and *deeds inrolled*, "which be in nature of fine, and whereupon wo-"men covert have been uſed to be examined, "taken, had or acknowledged, as well within "the city of London, as in many other cities, "boroughs and towns within the realm of Eng-"land, ſhould bind all ſuch women covert, that "ſhould happen to be examined upon the ſame "recoveries or deeds inrolled." It is therefore enacted, "That all recoveries, deeds inrolled, and "releaſes heretofore acknowledged and taken, or "at any time hereafter to be taken and acknow-"ledged before the mayors, aldermen, recorders, "chamberlains, or other head officer or officers, "as well of the city of London, as of any other "city, borough, or town corporate, within the "realm of England, having power and authority "to take and receive the ſame, according to the "laudable uſages and cuſtoms of the ſaid cities, "boroughs, and towns; and every of them ſhall "be and remain of the like force, ſtrength and "effect," &c. as before *this ſtatute*."

(*a*) Brook *faits inrolled*, pl. 15.
(*b*) 27 H. 8.

That

That the inrolment of deeds was very ancient, appears from many inſtances in the books. The 27th of H. 8. which requires every bargain and ſale of lands for a pecuniary conſideration to be inrolled within ſix months after its date, did not introduce into uſage or law the inrolment of deeds; but only enacted, that no ſuch bargain and ſale ſhould be valid, unleſs inrolled within the time before limited. And this proviſion by the 5th Eliz. c. 26. was extended to the courts of the counties palatine of Cheſter, Lancaſter, and Durham. It is obſervable, that not one of thoſe ſtatutes ſays any thing of the acknowledgment of the deed by a party to it, before a judge or magiſtrate; for it is now generally underſtood, that the neceſſity of an acknowledgment *was owing to the common law*, which, as it would not admit the voluntary inrolment of a deed, even for ſafe cuſtody, *without acknowledgment*, much leſs would it permit a deed to be inrolled by virtue of this ſtatute, without acknowledgment or ſomething equivalent unto it: from thence it clearly follows, that *inrolment of deeds was by common law.*

In a manuſcript report of the caſe of *Smartle* v. *Williams*, Paſch. 6 William and Mary, by counſel in the cauſe (*a*), it is ſaid the plaintiff, (not having the original deed, which was a mortgage for a term of 500 years) "gave in evidence a copy "of it inrolled in Chancery, upon acknowledg- "ment before a maſter there; and held, *per Cu-* "*riam*, good evidence, being an acknowledgment "of the party; and no difference between this and "a bargain and ſale inrolled: for though the ſta- "tute requires inrolment, yet it doth not make "the inrolment more evidence, than in the other "caſe; and *inrolment of deeds was at common* "*law.*"

(*a*) Lev. 3. ſec. 387.

*Acknow-*

## *Acknowledgment of Deeds by common Law.*

We fee as early as in the 21ft year of Edward the 3d (*a*), that a woman brought error to reverfe the inrolment of a deed of releafe made by her hufband and herfelf of all her right in certain lands, and affigned for error, that the Court had inrolled the deed by her acknowledgment, who was then covert, whereas they had not power to examine her without writ: and in the (*b*) 44th of the fame king, the lord of Tiptoft came into court, to have a deed of feoffment to the lord Walter Huet inrolled; and the Court finding on examination, that livery had not been made, would not permit it to be inrolled till that was done. In this cafe we even fee, that, to the notoriety of livery and feifin, they fuperadded that of inrolment, where land was paffed by deed. In the (*c*) 7th of Edward 4th, one came to Littleton (*d*), and "prayed an obligation might be inrolled: Little-"ton examined him, as to his knowledge of the "contents and his age, telling him, if it was in-"rolled, he could not deny the deed, or fay that "he was not of age, or that it was made by du-"refs: but he agreeing to the inrolment, it was "inrolled." In this inftance, the inrolment was not of a deed paffing land, but only of a bond, which now the law does not require to be inrolled. And yet a *recognizance* muft be inrolled; for the acknowledgment of it before a judge *gives it the force of a record*, though the inrolment of it be neceffary for the teftification and perpetuating of it.

(*a*) Br. *faits inrolled*, pl. 3.
(*b*) Br. *ibidem*.
(*c*) Br. *ibid.* pl. 11.
(*d*) It appears, from Dugdale, that Littleton was a judge of the common pleas in the 6th year of Edw[d] the 4th.

it (*a*). Statutes merchant and of the ſtaple are holden to be effectual againſt executors without inrolment: but againſt purchaſers of the conuſor's land, they are not of force, unleſs inrolled within three months from their date. (*b*) And Lord Coke, 2 Inſt. 673, ſays, "A deed acknowledged by huſband and wife "ſhall *by the common law be inrolled* only for "him, and if inrolled for both it binds her not;" and gives the reaſon before mentioned, "that "none have power to examine her without writ."

I think I need ſay nothing more to prove, that the common law of this country authoriſes and warrants the inrolment of deeds. There cannot, however, be any higher authority to prove this poſition, than an act of parliament paſſed in the 6th year of Richard II. c. 4. which is above four hundred years ago, viz. in the year 1382. This ſtatute enacts, that all deeds inrolled, which had been deſtroyed in the then late inſurrection, being exemplified, ſhould have the force and effect of the originals. It is to be obſerved, that the ſtatute ſpeaks of a general uſage and cuſtom, not of a rare ſcarce practice; it ſays, *all inrolments of deeds and other muniments inrolled in any of the four courts of record*; in ſome of which, it is more than probable, that the greateſt part, if not all deeds affecting the titles of lands were in thoſe days inrolled.

It would admit of much argument, though of no important conſequence, to diſcuſs the point, whether the common law did or did not require the inrolment of every deed, and how, in proceſs of time, this requiſition became relaxed, or the uſage diſpenſed with. It is ſufficiently evident, from the inſtances adduced, that the principles and reaſons, upon which the common law either re-

(*a*) Hob. 196. Hall v. Winchfield.
(*b*) Went. of Executors, 159.

quired or allowed of the inrolment of deeds, are ſuch as evince, in the preſent day, the neceſſary exigency of an univerſal inrolment.

### *Of the Inrolment of Deeds by Statute.*

Sir M. Hale ſays, that (*a*) "it was the great "deſign of the ſtatute of 27th H. 8, to have "brought about that method of aſſurance; and if "it had been purſued, it had before this time been "brought to great perfection, and done much of "that good, which is now intended by it."

We have already ſaid ſo much about this ſtatute, that it will be uſeleſs to repeat the reaſons of its having paſſed into a law, or of the effects of that law.

### *Effects of inrolling Deeds.*

There are ſome effects to be found in the books produced by the inrolment of deeds, which I have not as yet noticed; for inſtance, (*b*) "a "deed to lead the uſes of a fine of the eſtate of "the wife; the maſter of the Rolls was againſt ad-"mitting a copy of the inrolment, and made a "diſtinction that the inrolment of a *bargain and* "*ſale (by ſtatute)* is a record, but a deed for ſafe "cuſtody might be ſaid to be recorded: yet on an "iſſue directed by lord keeper, the chief juſtice "admitted it in evidence." And in the before-mentioned caſe of *Smartle* v. *Williams*, (3 Lev. 387) on a trial at bar, "a copy of a mortgage-"deed" (which was not a bargain and ſale according to the ſtatute) "was admitted, and the Court "ſaid the acknowledgment binds the party and "all claiming under him."

(*a*) Sir M. Hale's tract on the benefit of regiſtering deeds, p. 36.

(*b*) 2 Vern. 471. 591.

I can-

I cannot here forbear repeating an obſervation, which I before made, that the ſubject of theſe ſheets had never been thoroughly inveſtigated, maturely conſidered, nor ſettled in any regular conſiſtency. From the precedents that I have quoted, it not only appears, that a copy of a bargain and ſale inrolled according to the ſtatute of Henry VIII. but even of any other deed inrolled, whether for ſafe cuſtody or otherwiſe, may be produced in evidence: but if this were ſuch poſitive and certain law, whence then aroſe the neceſſity of paſſing the before-mentioned act of the ſixth of Richard II. for if office copies were evidence of deeds inrolled, why needed they to be exemplified under the great ſeal to make them evidence? And again, much nearer to our own days, the following part of the tenth of Queen Ann, c. 18. ſec. 3. muſt either prove the law to be otherwiſe, or it is perfectly uſeleſs and redundant: " and for ſupplying a fail-" ure in pleading or deriving the title to lands, " tenements or hereditaments, conveyed by deeds " of bargain and ſale, indented and inrolled ac-" cording to the ſtatute made in the twenty-ſeventh " year of the reign of King Henry VIII. for in-" rolment of bargains and ſales, where the original " indentures of bargain and ſale to be ſhewed forth " or produced, are wanting, which often happens, " eſpecially where divers lands, tenements or here-" ditaments are comprized in the ſame indenture, " and afterwards derived to ſeveral perſons: Be it " further enacted by the authority aforeſaid, that " wherein any declaration, avowry, bar, replication " or other pleading whatſoever, any ſuch indenture " of bargain and ſale inrolled, ſhall be pleaded " with a *profert in curia*, or offer to produce the " ſame, the perſon or perſons ſo pleading, ſhall " and may produce and ſhew forth, and be ſuf-" fered and allowed to produce and ſhew forth,

" by the authority of this act, to anſwer ſuch *pro-* " *fert*, as well againſt her Majeſty, her heirs and " ſucceſſors, as againſt any other perſon or perſons, " a copy of the inrolment of ſuch bargain and " ſale, and ſuch copy examined with the inrol- " ment, and ſigned by the proper officer, having " the cuſtody of ſuch inrolment, and proved upon " oath to be a true copy, ſo examined and ſigned, " ſhall be of the ſame force and effect, to all in- " tents and conſtructions of law, as the ſaid in- " dentures of bargain and ſale were and ſhould " be of, if the ſame were in ſuch caſe produced " and ſhewn forth."

To follow up the obſervation; we muſt not forget that it is holden, that *the acknowledgment binds the party acknowledging, and all claiming under him:* and yet it is ſaid in (*a*) *Taylor* v. *Jones*, " If two " are parties to a deed, and one acknowledges it " before a judge, it binds the other; and if a " man lives in New England, and would paſs land " here, they join a nominal party with him in the " deed, who acknowledges, and it binds." Now, if we do but reflect one moment upon the reaſon, nature and effect of an inrolment, we ſhall find, that *the acknowledgment, which* is the warrant to the officer to inrol the deed, is nothing more nor leſs, than an avowal by the granting party, that the deed which he has executed is his own act and deed; and that he thus ſolemnly deſires it may be from thenceforth rendered notorious, and perpetuated as a record of the court, for the purpoſe of manifeſting, maintaining and eſtabliſhing the title. Now, what can ſo ſtrongly inſult common ſenſe (and what elſe ſhould all law and equity ſpring from or be reduced to) as to be taught,

(*a*) 1 Salk. 270.

that

that the (*a*) *inrolment of a deed is to no other purpose, but that the party ſhall not deny it afterwards*; and that the acknowledgment of a mere nominal party, who in fact is neither grantor nor grantee, *ſhall bind*, and make the inrolment valid: for to what good, or even miſchievous purpoſe ſhall a mere nominal party deny a deed?

Again it is holden, (*b*) *that againſt a deed* inrolled, a man may plead infancy, although none can plead *non eſt factum*; and yet why ſhould the acknowledgment by a mere nominal party, or by a grantee, prevent the grantor, (whom I ſuppoſe totally ignorant of the acknowledgment and ſubſequent inrolment) from pleading *non eſt factum*, after ſuch inrolment, more than if the deed had not been inrolled? After ſuch glaring inconſiſtencies, it would be too abſurd to deny, that the law ought to be amended and improved.

Before I entirely quit this ſubject, it will not be improper to call the attention of my readers to the inattention and ignorance of parliament concerning the law of inrolment. The 21ſt Jam. I. c. 26, after reciting, "that many lewd perſons of baſe "condition, uſed to acknowledge deeds in the "name of others, not privy nor conſenting to "the ſame, which hath and daily doth turn to the "great charge, trouble and undoing of many of "the good ſubjects of this kingdom, and rather "for that there is no remedy in law to reform "theſe and the like abuſes;" enacts, "That all "perſon or perſons acknowledging or procuring "to be acknowledged, any deed or deeds inrolled "in the name of any other perſon or perſons not "privy or conſenting to the ſame, and being "thereof lawfully convicted or attainted, ſhall be

(*a*) Viner. Inrolm. E. 3, pag. 445.
(*b*) 2 Lev. 65. Sir W. Pelham's caſe.

" adjudged, eſteemed, and taken to be felons, " and ſuffer the pains of death," &c. Now if, as we have ſeen, the acknowledgment binds the acknowledging party and all claiming under him, and the inrolment binds only, when the deed hath been acknowledged, (even by a nominal party) I beg to be informed, what miſchievous effects can be produced by the acknowledgment of a deed in the name of another *perſon not privy nor conſenting to the ſame:* for it is evident, that ſuch perſon is a ſtranger to the deed, as well as to the inrolment of it, and therefore utterly incapable of giving or taking away its validity and effect. It is then certain, that the framers of this act, neither attended to nor underſtood the nature, operation and effects of acknowledging and inrolling deeds, &c. &c.

*Of the Inrolment of Roman Catholics Deeds.*

The next time the legiſlature thought proper to interfere or paſs any law concerning the inrolment of deeds, was upon the ſpur of the times; to anſwer a particular purpoſe, and produce a particular effect. This was to render notorious and public every act and deed, by which a catholic paſſed, altered or changed his landed property. For, by the 3d Geo. I. c. 18, it is enacted, " That " from and after the twenty-ninth day of September in the year 1717, no manors, lands, tenements, " hereditaments, or any intereſt therein, or rent or " profit thereout, ſhall paſs, alter or change from " any papiſt or perſon profeſſing the popiſh religion, by any deed or will, except ſuch deed " within ſix months after the date, and ſuch will " within ſix months after the death of the teſtator, " be inrolled in one of the king's courts of record " at Weſtminſter, or elſe within the ſame county " or counties wherein the manors, lands and tene-

" ments

" ments lie, by the custos rotulorum and two " justices of the peace, and the clerk of the peace " of the same county or counties, or two of them " at the least, whereof the clerk of the peace to " be one." An act almost annually passes, for *allowing further time for inrolment of deeds and wills made by papists, and for the relief of protestant purchasers.* As this act of Geo. I. is of much utility and importance in the prosecution of my present researches, I shall premise some general observations upon its nature, tendency and operation, before I enter into the legal effects of it, with respect to the law of inrolment.

This is one of the many penal laws now in force against the Roman catholic subjects of this country. It is a *penal* law, because it was intended to impose a burthen upon the professors of that religion, to which their fellow subjects were not liable; and to deter them in future from offences, of which they were then presumed guilty.

It is obvious, that before a man can give title to another, he must have a title himself: *Nemo dat, quod non habet.* A man cannot have land himself, if he be by law incapacitated *to have or to hold it.* By our laws, there are but two methods of acquiring landed property in this country: one by descent, when the law casts the inheritance upon the heir at law, after the death of the ancestor; the other by purchase, which includes every acquisition of land under a gift, deed or will. Now when this act of the 3d Geo. I. passed, the legislature could not, or at least ought not, to have been ignorant of the 11th and 12th of William III. c. 4, by which every person educated in the popish religion, or professing the same, is absolutely " *disabled and " made incapable to inherit or take by descent, devise, " or limitation in possession, reversion or remainder, " any lands, tenements or hereditaments* within the

 kingdom

" kingdom of England, dominion of Wales, and " town of Berwick upon Tweed, and is alſo *dis-" abled and made incapable to purchaſe either in his " or her own name, or in the name of any other per-" ſon or perſons, to his or her uſe, or in truſt for him " or her, any manors, lands or profits out of lands, " tenements, rents, terms or hereditaments,* within " the kingdom of England, dominion of Wales, " and town of Berwick upon Tweed, and that " *all and ſingular eſtates, terms, and any other " intereſts and profits whatſoever out of lands,* " from and after the ſaid 10th day of April " (viz. 1700) *made, ſuffered or done to or for the " uſe or behoof of any ſuch perſon or perſons, or upon " any truſt or confidence mediately or immediately to or " for the benefit or relief of any ſuch perſon or perſons, " ſhall be utterly void and of none effect to all intents, " conſtructions and purpoſes whatſoever.*"

Can words be more obvious, explicit, and concluſive? If then a perſon educated in or profeſſing the Roman catholic religion, can neither take land by deſcent nor purchaſe, he cannot take it at all: if he cannot take, he cannot hold; for *prius eſt habere quàm tenere.* An alien may take land by purchaſe: but he cannot hold it, but for the benefit of the crown. If he cannot have, he cannot give. How abſurd and repugnant then is it to enact, that no deed nor deviſe of land by a Roman catholic, ſhall be good and valid, unleſs inrolled within ſix months: for the conſequence evidently is, *therefore, if ſo inrolled, it ſhall be good and valid.* That this was the intent and ſenſe of the legiſlature is ſufficiently clear, from the conſtant uſage of inrolling all ſuch deeds and wills, which have often been controverted and eſtabliſhed as valid in the courts of law and equity.

If this act of 3d Geo. I. can operate at all, it muſt be by virtually repealing the 11th and 12th of Wil. and the fires in London, in the year 1780, were

were very flagrant proofs, that the 11th and 12th of Wil. III. till that time was generally underſtood to be unrepealed and in full force. In the caſe of *Pelham* and *Fletcher* (*a*), " a Papiſt aſſigned to a " proteſtant for a full conſideration: an ejectment " was brought againſt the aſſignee by a ſubſequent " mortgagee, who recovered by the diſability of " the firſt mortgagee. (*b*) All this appeared upon a " bill brought in Chancery; and my lord chancel- " lor was of opinion, that *a mortgage to a papiſt is* " *void* (*c*). But in this caſe, the aſſignment to " the proteſtant, and the trial in ejectment, were " both before the 3d of Geo. I." (that is, the ſtatute for inrolling the deeds of Papiſts) " which " were it otherwiſe, would it ſeems have made " an alteration." And what other alteration, but by removing the diſability of the papiſt, and conſequently virtually repealing the 11th and 12th Wil. III. by which the diſability was created.

*The Inconſiſtency of theſe two penal Laws.*

If we take a complex view of theſe two acts, the repreſentation will be faithfully this: A papiſt, who, by the act of Wil. can neither take land by *deſcent nor purchaſe*, may, by the act of Geo. I. give or deviſe it away by deed or will inrolled. What can more efficiently do away every effect of the ſtatute of Wil. III. than the 3d of Geo. I. and all the ſubſequent acts, by which the lands poſſeſſed by Catholics are ſubjected to a double landtax, and to a regiſtry, and are almoſt annually affected by the act for *allowing further time for inrolment of deeds and wills made by papiſts, and for the relief of proteſtant purchaſers?*

(*a*) 3 New Abr. 709, Michaelmas 1729.

(*b*) For being, as a papiſt, diſabled to take the land himſelf, he could not aſſign it to another.

(*c*) Viner recuſant, 263.

It

It is ſelf-evident, that lands which are poſſeſſed by a Catholic, muſt have been taken by the poſſeſſor, either by deſcent or purchaſe; for there is no other mode of taking lands: and by the act of Wil. III. he is made abſolutely *incapable of taking lands by deſcent or purchaſe.* Either therefore the act of Geo. I. with every ſubſequent annual act relative to the ſame ſubject, is an abſolute nullity, as grounded upon an impoſſible ſuppoſition, viz. *that a Catholic could take land by deſcent or purchaſe, ſince the paſſing of the act of Wil. III.* or theſe latter acts completely do away the effects of the act of Wil. III. by enabling papiſts to take land by deſcent or purchaſe. And I put theſe queſtions impartially to every man. Did the Roman Catholics obtain any relief by the repeal of that part of King William's act? In what could that relief conſiſt, but in acquiring a capacity, which they had not before, of taking lands by deſcent or purchaſe? It is one amidſt many ſtriking inſtances of the blind and inconſiderate judgment of the public, when we throw our eyes back to the ferments and riots, that ſet London in a blaze in the year 1780, merely becauſe the legiſlature had repealed in expreſs words, what had in fact been virtually repealed from the year 1717. For by this act of repeal paſſed in the 20th year of his preſent Majeſty, a Roman Catholic may now take land by deſcent or purchaſe, which he may ſettle, charge, mortgage, ſell or give away by deed or will inrolled: and by the 3d Geo. I. he was enabled to ſettle, charge, mortgage, ſell or give away his land, by deed or will inrolled; which he could not do without taking the land: what then can a Roman Catholic do more under the expreſs repeal of that part of King William's act by the 20th of his preſent Majeſty, than he before could under the virtual repeal of it by the 3d Geo. I.?

The inconſiſtencies of theſe penal ſtatutes run to

an extent exceeding all credibility. For will any man ſuppoſe it poſſible, that the wiſdom of the Britiſh legiſlature ſhould declare in the ſame ſpirit and intention, and by written laws, meant to ſubſiſt and be inforced together, and with a view and expreſs reference to each other (*a*), that a papiſt not having taken a particular oath preſcribed by the 30th of Charles II. is rendered abſolutely incapable of taking land by deſcent or purchaſe (*b*): and that every papiſt ſhall take this very oath at the age of twenty-one years or within ſix months after his coming *into poſſeſſion of any lands or rents out of lands*, or ſhall regiſter the eſtate *into the poſſeſſion of which he has come* in the manner ſpecified in the act, under the penalty of forfeiting the fee-ſimple thereof; two thirds to the king, and one third to the informer? Can folly and abſurdity be more glaring? Firſt to require an oath to be taken at the age of eighteen, and then to annex the incapacity of taking the land to the noncompliance with that requiſition; and afterwards to require the ſame oath to be taken at the age of twenty-one, or ſix months after a perſon comes into poſſeſſion of *what he cannot take*; and to annex the forfeiture of that very land, *which he cannot take*, to the king and informer, for his neglecting to regiſter the ſame after he *has taken* it.

*Inconveniences of the 3d of Geo. I.*

The act requires every deed and will to be inrolled within ſix months from the date thereof, but makes no proviſion for either a deed or will executed out of the nation, which frequently cannot by poſſibility be inrolled within the time limited: it directs the deed to be inrolled, yet it neither expreſſes whether it ſhall be inrolled by acknowledg-

(*a*) 11 & 12th Wil. 3d. (*b*) 3 Geo. 1ſt.

ment

ment or *fiat*, or whether a copy of the inrolment ſhall be admitted in evidence. If effect were to be given to the act of Wil. III. by really incapacitating a Roman Catholic from taking lands by deſcent or purchaſe; theſe latter conſiderations could not affect them: but they are of infinite conſequence to proteſtant purchaſers; for ſuppoſing, that under a deed or will executed by a catholic owner of land at Bengal, a Proteſtant ſhould become intitled, to the prejudice of the heir at law; would it not be a hard caſe on one hand, that an heir at law ſhould be diſinherited by an inſtrument, which under an expreſs act of parliament is null and void; and on the other hand, that a purchaſer ſhould be defeated in his rights, for the omiſſion of a condition impoſed by act of parliament, which it was impoſſible to perform?

### *Unconſtitutional Hardſhip of the Third of George the Firſt.*

An unprecedented hardſhip attends this act, which muſt upon conſideration appear wholly unconſtitutional; for by it a man is compelled by a public act recorded in court, to avow and confeſs himſelf guilty of a crime, which draws upon him the very extreme rigor of the law, in the penalties of premunire, outlawry, felony and treaſon; to which every one knows, that the profeſſion of the Roman catholic religion ſubjects its votaries. The very acknowledgment of the neceſſity of inrolling a deed under this ſtatute is *ipſo facto* an avowal of a perſon's being a Roman Catholic. Let us hear the language and doctrine of our courts upon this matter (*a*): "A bill was brought, praying, " that defendant might diſcover whether I. S.

(*a*) 3 New. Abr. 799. Trin. 12th G. 2. Smith v. Read.

" (under

" (under whose will the defendant claimed) was a " papist or not. The defendant pleaded the statute " of the eleventh and twelfth William III. and the " Lord Chancellor was of opinion, that he was not " obliged to discover; that there is no rule better " established, than, *that a man shall not be obliged* " *to answer, to what may subject him to the penalty* " *of an act of parliament*, and there can be no doubt, " but this is a penal law inflicting disabilities or " incapacities. If a bill is brought against the " person for discovery, whether he is a Papist or " not, he is not bound to discover; and where is " the difference between him and the person claim- " ing under him? Besides, what sways with me " very much is the great inconvenience that would " follow, should this plea be disallowed; we should " have nothing in this court but bills of discovery, " whether such and such persons were Papists or " not, and nobody knows what confusion would " follow, therefore the plea must be allowed." Is it not strange, that whilst the courts held such doctrine, the legislature should contrive, by a side wind and indirect compulsion, to force a *man to answer to what may subject him to the penalty of an act of parliament?* And *there is no doubt but this is a penal law.*

*Further Inconveniences of the 3d of George* I.

Besides the inconsistencies and hardships of the act, a very important inconveniency must ever certainly attend the execution of it. It certainly passed to the end (as the preamble expresses it) *that the estates of Papists may be certainly known and discovered.* Should not then the act have prescribed some method of ascertaining this crime of popery, which renders a person incapable of taking land by descent or purchase; or which requires the inrolment of all their deeds and wills, and have determined

determined a time (at leaſt after the deaths of the parties) after which, the proof of this incapacity or requiſition ſhould be precluded? It will be readily admitted, that the legiſlature, by *making known and diſcovered the eſtates of Papiſts*, and by paſſing annual acts for the relief of proteſtant purchaſers, never could have meant or intended to render the titles of Papiſts (if a perſon unable to take land by deſcent or purchaſe can have title) to their lands *dubious and uncertain*. And it is clear to demonſtration, that every title muſt be dubious and uncertain, which depends upon a condition or requiſition, the neceſſity of which is created by ſtatute, but of which no legal evidence can be procured or produced.

*A ſuppoſed Caſe before the Repeal of any Part of the Act of King William III.*

A conveyancer knows, that by one act of parliament a Papiſt is incapacitated to take land either by deſcent or purchaſe; and that by another act, no deed nor will affecting land made by a Papiſt is good, unleſs inrolled within ſix months. An abſtract of a title is brought to him to peruſe on behalf of a purchaſer of a Papiſt's land. The firſt thing to be attended to is, how this fact (which is the ſtigma guilt or crime of popery) can be proved or eſtabliſhed; for upon that, the whole title hinges. The omiſſion to inrol ſome leading deed is ſtated. How ſhall a man after his death be proved not to have conformed to the eſtabliſhed church, or to have diſſented from it? And yet if a perſon educated in or profeſſing the popiſh religion, be incapable of taking by deſcent or purchaſe, (and conſequently of tranſmiting, limiting, or ſelling); or if the act of William be rendered a nullity, by the virtual repeal of the 3d Geo. I. or if it loſe its efficacy from its own abſurdity or inconſiſtency,

consiſtency, or from the preſumption and tacit agreement of the nation collectively and individually; or if the deed or will of a Papiſt (who in ſpite of that act may have taken an eſtate by deſcent or purchaſe) be without inrolment an abſolute nullity; how can ſuch a title be approved of? And if doubted, how can the ambiguity be done away? For the conformity or nonconformity with the eſtabliſhed church in this caſe creates the capacity or incapacity to take, and the obligation or nonobligation to inrol; upon which depends the validity or nullity of the deed, and conſequently that of the title.

It is a ſubject of aſtoniſhment, notwithſtanding the groſs, palpable and pointed contradiction of theſe acts, how catholic landed property has been preſerved in the very few, who ſtill profeſs the tenets of that belief; and ſtill more, how titles to mortgagees and purchaſers have been daily made out, deduced through, and from perſons labouring under the firſt of all defects in a title, viz. an abſolute incapacity to take land either by deſcent or purchaſe.

## *Unintended Effects of repealing a Part of King William's Act.*

We are more to commend the liberality, than admire the wiſdom of the parliament, which repealed that part of the act of King William, that diſabled a Roman Catholic to take land by deſcent or purchaſe. In reſolving to remove the incapacity, they had not the precaution to provide againſt the inconſiſtencies, which muſt neceſſarily attend a partial alteration of the law. There cannot be a doubt, but that the 3d of George I. is and was intended to be a penal law, and a hardſhip impoſed upon the Roman Catholics; for the preamble ſtates the reaſon of its paſſing, viz. " in order that " they

"they may be deterred (if poffible) from the like "offences for the future." It is well known, that the inrolment of deeds is attended with an expence for additional ftamps, for entering them on the rolls, and for the fees of office; another reafon, why fuch deeds and wills by Catholics are inrolled was and is "to *render public and notorious the* "*eftates of papifts.*" Behold now the perverfion of all thefe ends! A Proteftant purchafes land from a Papift, (and (*a*) now a Papift can take by defcent or purchafe, and therefore may fell:) the purchafe deed is to be inrolled; the expence of a purchafe deed, without a fpecial contrary agreement, is always upon the purchafer; the Proteftant then pays the expences, and the Proteftant's eftate is rendered public and notorious; and thus whatever hardfhip, expence or inconveniency, was intended to be impofed upon the Roman Catholic, is in fact transferred from him to the Proteftant: and at prefent, as a Roman Catholic may legally purchafe, the deed, by which the Proteftant conveys the land to him, needs not to be inrolled; and the Catholic may take under fuch a deed, either without any fuch expence or notoriety of title, to which the proteftant purchafer is fubject.

### *Experimental Effects of the 3d of George I.*

In whatever light we view this ftatute, there appear the moft cogent reafons for repealing it. It has however produced fome effects, which form an experiment, how an univerfal inrolment act would tend to fimplify and improve the law.

If we may be permitted to drop the ideas of incongruity and contradiction, which I have before mentioned, refult from the ftatutes firft difabling, then virtually enabling Papifts to take land, and

(*a*) 20 Geo. III.

lastly

lastly qualifying and admitting their possession and seisin; we may argue from their possessing, passing and changing their lands from the year 1717 to the present day, in the same manner, as if the 11th and 12th of William had in fact never been made. In this supposition, the title of a Roman Catholic to his land is ever more sure, clear and certain from that period, than the title of a Protestant; and the statute gives the obvious reasons for it, viz. the Catholic's estate is thereby (*a*) *certainly known and discovered*; and for this reason have their lands in several instances borne a higher price in the market, than those of their neighbours; nor will this be found unreasonable, when we reflect, that the establishment of a registery with all its imperfections and inconveniences, certainly raises the value of land in the counties of York and Middlesex above the rate, at which land of a similar quality, will sell at in a neighbouring county, and secure a preference in landed securities given for money in those counties over others. The truth of this daily appears from the advertisements for sales and loans in the newspapers.

The necessary inference from these premises is, that by how much more clear the title of a land-owner is to his estate, of so much more value is it to a purchaser: and by how much more readily he can raise money upon it, of so much more value is it to himself. The prices of land and of the funds must always keep pace with each other, and by them the prosperity and credit of the nation may be always ascertained. The disabling part of the 11th and 12th of William is now expressly repealed by the 20th of his present Majesty; but till that had been done, it was whimsically unaccountable to reflect, that one statute, enacted as a penal

(*a*) Preamble of 1st Geo. I. s. 2.

law against the Roman Catholics, should have been in practice and in fact wholly disregarded, and another most strictly observed. For few, if any, persons ever thought of giving force to the act of William, or of neglecting the requisition of 3d of George I. (*a*).

*The Decisions of the Courts upon the Act of King William.*

Having said so much of the inconsistency and repugnancy of the two acts of Will. III. and Geo. I. it behoves me to prove my positions, by shewing the decisions of the courts upon them. I do it with that submission and deference, which is due to the authority of our supreme courts: it must be remembered at the same time, that these decisions are, upon that part of an act, which is now repealed; and I quote them, with a view and intention of proving, that another act ought to be repealed.

He, who runs, may read the intent and meaning of the 4th section of 11th and 12th Will. III. c. 4. "And be it also further enacted, by the authority "aforesaid, that from and after the nine and twen-"tieth day of September, which shall be in the year "of our Lord one thousand seven hundred, if any "person educated in the popish religion, or pro-"fessing the same, shall not, within six months, af-"ter he or she shall attain the age of eighteen years, "take the oaths of allegiance and supremacy, and "also subscribe the declaration set down and ex-"pressed in an act of parliament made in the "thirtieth year of the reign of the late King

(*a*) I find this observation sanctioned by Bishop Barnet, in the History of his own Time, Vol. II. p. 229; where, after setting forth the inconsistent severity of this act, he concludes in these words, "*So this act was not followed nor executed in any* "*sort.*"

"Charles

" Charles II. intituled, *An act for the more effectual preserving the king's person and government, by disabling Papists from sitting in either house of parliament*, to be by him or her made, repeated and subscribed in the courts of Chancery or King's Bench, or quarter sessions of the county, where such person shall reside, every such person shall, in respect of him or herself only, and not to or in respect of any of his or her heirs or posterity, be disabled and made incapable to inherit, or take by descent, devise or limitation, in possession, reversion or remainder, any lands, tenements or hereditaments within the kingdom of England, dominion of Wales, or town of Berwick upon Tweed: And that during the life of such person, or until he or she do take the said oaths, and make, repeat, and subscribe the said declaration in manner as aforesaid, the next of his or her kindred, which shall be a Protestant, shall have and enjoy the said lands, tenements and hereditaments, without being accountable for the profits by him or her received during such enjoyment thereof, as aforesaid: but in case of any wilful waste committed on the said lands, tenements or hereditaments, by the person so having or enjoying the same, or any other by his or her licence or authority, the party disabled, his or her executors and administrators, shall and may recover treble damages for the same, against the person committing such waste, his or her executors or administrators, by action of debt in any of his Majesty's courts of record at Westminster; and that from and after the tenth day of April, which shall be in the year of our Lord one thousand seven hundred, every Papist or person making profession of the popish religion shall be disabled, and is hereby made incapable to purchase either in his or her own name, or in

" the name of any other perſon or perſons to his
" or her uſe, or in truſt for him or her, any manors,
" lands, profits out of lands, tenements, rents,
" terms or hereditaments, within the kingdom of
" England, dominion of Wales, and town of Ber-
" wick upon Tweed; and that all and ſingular
" eſtates, terms, and any other intereſts or profits
" whatſoever out of lands, from and after the ſaid
" tenth day of April, to be made, ſuffered or done
" to or for the uſe or behoof of any ſuch perſon
" or perſons, or upon any truſt or confidence, me-
" diately or immediately, to or for the benefit or
" relief of any ſuch perſon or perſons, ſhall be ut-
" terly void and of none effect, to all intents, con-
" ſtructions and purpoſes whatſoever."

In confirmation of the obvious meaning and intent of this ſtatute, which indubitably was to hinder Roman Catholics from taking or poſſeſſing landed property, it has been ſolemnly determined (*a*), that " the perſons who were eighteen years
" old at the time of making the ſtatute of Wil-
" liam III. are within the intent and meaning,
" though out of the letter of the act; for it is re-
" markable, that this clauſe extends only to the caſe,
" where the papiſt is under the age of eighteen
" years at the time, that the lands come to him;
" but where the papiſt is above eighteen years of
" age when the land comes to him, he is utterly
" diſabled to take, and the eſtate is void" (*b*).
" Deviſe to a papiſt, is a purchaſe within this
" act" (*c*): and it is ſettled, " that either a de-
" viſe or ſettlement to a perſon profeſſing the po-
" piſh religion of above eighteen years and ſix
" months of age, is *void*, and the perſon not capa-

(*a*) 9 Mod. 35. Trin. 9. G. Carrick v. Errington.
(*b*) Wm. Rep. 254. Trin. 1717. Vane v. Fletcher.
(*c*) 9 Mod. 170. Roper v. Ratcliffe, in the Houſe of Lords.

" ble

" ble of taking: the act intending utterly to disable " the papist of that age to take any new acquisition, *or what was not his ancient inheritance*" (*a*). The statute extends to trusts as well as legal estates, and to a term of years, or even for six months, as well as to a freehold or an inheritance, and " the " trust of a term is as much within the act as the " legal interest of a term (*b*)."

It appears, that these decisions upon the incapacity of a papist acquiring any land by purchase either under a deed or will, are strictly consonant with the words, spirit and meaning of the act: but what judgment are we to form of the decisions made upon the other words of the act, *be disabled and made incapable to inherit, or take by descent, devise or limitation in possession, reversion or remainder any lands*, &c.? The singularity of these decisions will scarcely be credited.

To inherit or take by descent is certainly to take by operation of law, and not by the act of the party (*c*). " Lord Dover being possessed of a " long term for years, made his will, and his lady, " who was a papist, executrix thereof. And it was " resolved by Lord Chancellor, that notwithstanding the disabling act of the 11th and 12th of " Will. III. the term vested absolutely in her; and " this was not a purchase within that act. And " he said, that a papist may be a tenant in dower " or by the curtesy; because, in all these cases, it " is by *operation of law, and not by the act of the* " *party*, that the estate comes to him." It requires some slight knowledge of the law to perceive the distinction between an executor taking a chattel interest (such as is a term of years) as executor, and a person's taking the same interest under

(*a*) 2 Wm. Rep. 4, 5. (*b*) 9 Mod. 192.
(*c*) 3 New Ab. 799. case of Lord Dover's Will, and Vin. title Papist.

a devise or deed. Whatever a man inherits or takes by descent, must be a freehold and inheritance, not a chattel interest or term for years. In a statute so highly penal, the Court very humanely and liberally in this instance, (if I may be allowed the expression) invented this evasion of the severity of the law: but why it should not adhere to the spirit of the law, and go beyond its strict letter, in this instance, as well as it did in declaring that persons of eighteen years and a half old at the time of the making of the statute, were within the intent and meaning, though out of the letter of the law, I cannot command ingenuity enough to account for. Common sense tells us, that the intent and meaning of the act was certainly to prevent a papist from acquiring any interest even for one year in land: and shall it be seriously presumed, that a protestant, possessed of a leasehold estate worth £.50,000, shall by law be enabled to leave that to a papist, by making him executor, which he cannot give or leave him by deed or specific devise? When a particular object is intended to be accomplished by the legislature, it is derogatory from its dignity, that the courts of law should invent and countenance such subterfuges and evasions of its intended effects. The virtual repeal of the 11th and 12th of Will. III. by the 3d Geo. I. and its express repeal by the 20th of his present Majesty justify this language.

The reason alledged for this determination, viz. that *it is by operation of law, and not by any act of the party, that the estate comes to him*, every body must perceive, applies most emphatically to every descent cast by law, and would therefore do away the first and chief part of this very statute, which disables a papist *to inherit or take by descent, devise or limitation*; for it is by operation of law, and not by any act of the party, that an estate

comes

comes to an heir, who takes by descent, to a devisee, who takes under a will, and to a purchaser who takes by limitation under a deed.

But the subsequent decisions upon these words of the act, *be disabled and made incapable to take by descent, devise or limitation*, are still more wonderful, than those, which we have already quoted (*a*). "The heir at law, though a Papist, is *capable to* "*take the inheritance*; for it is in him, though the "next Protestant of kin hath the pernancy of the "profits, till the other becomes a Protestant; nor "shall the next remainder-man take immediately, "till after the death of the Papist." Be it observed, how inconsistent and contradictory are the foregoing and the subsequent determinations (*b*): "Per *Cur.* 9 Mod. 34. Trin. 9. G. in the case of "*Carrick* v. *Errington* cited there, as settled in the "case of the Duchess of *Hamilton*;" Lord Chancellor King held, "That the remainder should take "effect presently, in the same manner, as if a re-"mainder were limited to a monk for life, or to "one that refuses to take, or if such remainder-"man had been dead, and no such limitation had "been."

I will end my observations upon this statute, and the decisions upon it, with the following repetition: *That the statute extends to trusts as well as legal estates.* Now observe with astonishment how the courts judge of this matter (*c*). Per Pratt, Ch. Justice, "If Papists take conveyances to their "own trustees, and if it be undiscovered, all is "well; or if it be discovered, the conveyance, it "is true, is void by the act; but then it revests "again in the first owner or trustees." I cannot

(*a*) 9 Mod. 34 Trin. 9 Geo. Carrick v. Errington, and Roper and Ratcliff, ubi supra.

(*b*) 2 Wm. Rep. 362. Trin. 1726, Carrick v. Errington.

(*c*) 9 Mod. 194. Roper v. Ratcliff.

discover any words in the act, which either implicitly or explicitly import, that the disability of a Papist taking a trust estate, depends upon the discovery of its being a popish trust. The *non-discovery* of the *cestuy que trust*, certainly never can give validity to a conveyance, which was void *ab initio*; nor can there be a revesting, without a divesting: and nothing can divest by a conveyance, but what thereby moves out of the grantor: but here the conveyance was void, and therefore no effect can be given to it; and consequently nothing could thereby have moved out of the grantor. Again (*a*), "the act of 11th and 12th Will. III. is a bare "disability; it creates only a disability, but makes "no forfeiture; it prevents a vesting, but divests "nothing that is vested."

Another curious doctrine has been established by the courts, which appears upon reflection equally incompatible with the statute, which incapacitates a papist to *inherit or take land by descent, devise or limitation*.

(*b*) "The word *purchase* in this statute is only "a modification of the estate, and shall not be "taken in the full extent of the word; for those "purchases are intended only by the statute, by "which papists enlarge and extend their landed "interest, and not where by deeds of settlement, "the ancient family estate is new modelled, without making any new acquisition; so that even "at this day, a purchase by *limitation* in a settlement, or by devise to a papist under the age of "eighteen years, is good, so as such papist, within "six months after he comes to that age, conform "and take the oaths, &c, otherwise he loses the "pernancy of the profits during his life only."

(*a*) 9 Mod. 199. 200.
(*b*) 9 Mod. 180. Hil. 5 G. 1. Earl of Derwentwater's case.

The inconſiſtencies of this act and of the deciſions upon it, will appear leſs ſtrange, when we attend to the account which Biſhop Burnet gives of its paſſing. (a) " Thoſe who brought this into " the Houſe of Commons, hoped, that the court " would have oppoſed it; but the court promoted " the bill; ſo when the party ſaw their miſtake, " they ſeemed willing to let the bill fall; and when " that could not be done, they clogged it with " many ſevere and ſome unreaſonable clauſes, hop- " ing that the lords would not paſs the act; and " it was ſaid, that if the lords ſhould make the " leaſt alteration in it, they in the Houſe of Com- " mons, who had ſet it on, were reſolved to let it " lie on their table, when it ſhould be ſent back to " them. Many lords, who ſecretly favoured pa- " piſts, on the Jacobite account, did for this very " reaſon move for ſeveral alterations; ſome of " theſe importing a greater ſeverity; but the zeal " againſt popery was ſuch in that houſe, that the " bill paſſed without any amendment, and it had " the royal aſſent."

## *Of Inrolling Deeds by a Judge's Fiat.*

Before I leave this ſubject, I ſhall ſlightly touch upon a point of practice, which has attended the execution of this act of the 3d George I. It has been the general uſage to inrol all deeds under this act, not by acknowledgment of the execution by any of the parties to the deed, but by what is called a judge's *fiat*; (a) which in general is a

(a) Hiſtory of his own Time, 2d vol. p. 229.

(b) The Fiat is nothing more, than the ſignature of a judge to the following ſuperſcription on the face of the deed. *Let this deed be inrolled in the court of pursuant to the ſtatute, this day of* 178 A. B.

ſhort

ſhort order or warrant of ſome judge, for making out and allowing any certain proceſs, &c.

I have not been able to trace in the books the fainteſt idea of a deed being inrolled under a judge's *fiat*; ſuch however has been the general practice, which muſt appear truly ſurpriſing, when we throw back our recollection, to what is ſaid (in page 79 viz.) that *the neceſſity of an acknowledgment was owing to the common law*, which as it would not admit of the voluntary inrolment of a deed, even for ſafe cuſtody, without acknowledgment, much leſs would it permit a deed to be inrolled by virtue of a ſtatute without acknowledgment, or ſomething equivalent unto it. It cannot be queſtioned whether leſs formality and authority be required for the voluntary inrolment of a deed for ſafe cuſtody, or for the requiſite inrolment of a deed under a compulſory ſtatute. Upon what ground of authority then did the judges introduce and continue to iſſue theſe *fiats* for inrolment? It would be too hazardous to aſſert, that out of many thouſand deeds inrolled under *fiats*, not one is validly inrolled.

We have ſeen, that the *acknowledgment* of a deed to be inrolled under the ſtatute of Henry VIII. is previouſly requiſite for its inrolment, not by virtue of that ſtatute, but of the common law, (for the act ſays nothing of acknowledgment); ſo the ſtatute of George I. is equally ſilent as to the mode of inrolment. Either then a judge hath power to iſſue a warrant for inrolment by *fiat*, or he has not. If he hath power, it muſt be either by the prerogative of his office, or by written law. There is no mention made in any ſtatute, which hath come under my cognizance, of a judge's *fiat* for this purpoſe. If it be by common law or prerogative of office, it is paramount to the ſtatute of Henry VIII. but before that ſtatute, there was not known any diſtinction of inrolled deeds; that ſtatute required

the

the inrolment of a particular ſpecies of deed; but the mode of inrolling that particular ſpecies, did not vary from the mode of inrolling any other ſpecies of deed. The act directed no variation in this mode. The ſame reaſoning holds to the preſent day. The common law cannot be altered, but by an expreſs ſtatute; the judge's prerogative or power not having been extended or curtailed, as to any particular ſpecies of deed, it is one and the ſame over all. Upon what ground then, do they aſſume a power to iſſue *fiats* for inrolling deeds of Roman Catholics under the ſtatute of George I. which they diſavow and diſclaim for inrolling bargains and ſales under the ſtatute of Henry VIII. If this power ariſes by the common law, and the common law has never been altered by ſtatute, the judges certainly have equal power in both caſes. If they can iſſue a *fiat* for inrolling a deed in one, they can in every inſtance. For what is the inrolment of a deed? It is the act of a deed becoming either recorded in court, or a record of the court, according to what has been ſaid above; when it has been entered or ingroſſed upon a roll or ſcroll of parchment, ſuch ingroſſed copy ſhall not be recorded in the court, but by ſome warrant of a judge of the court, in which it is intended to be inrolled. This warrant is ſaid in the books to be the acknowledgment of the deed, to which the judge ſigns his name: (*a*) but as the deed cannot be entered or recorded in the court without a judge's name, ſo I muſt preſume, that every deed, to which a judge has ſigned his name by way of direction, order, warrant, authority, conſent or knowledge for

(*a*) The form of an acknowledgment is—*The execution of this deed was acknowledged by A. B. a party thereto before me, and was by him deſired to be inrolled in the court of*

A. B.

its

its inrolment, muſt after that, neceſſarily be entered or admitted as a record, by the officers of the court. They are bound by the judge's orders, which are to them mandatory and compulſive; the party, which is bound to procure the deed to be inrolled, can do no more, than to procure from a judge a direction, warrant, authority or order to the officer, to inrol the deed: the nature and mode of this direction, warrant, authority or order, muſt be immaterial to the officer and party; the latter is bound to comply with the requiſition of the ſtatute, which obliges him to inrol the deed, and the former will not, as he ought not, record any deed without the ſanction of a judge's name; and wherever a judge's direction, warrant, authority or order appears upon a deed, the officer cannot refuſe to record it, unleſs for a reaſon paramount to the authority of a judge, viz. for a parliamentary reaſon; ſuch for inſtance as is the want of a proper ſtamp. In ſuch caſe, although a deed be acknowledged or hath a *fiat*, yet if it be not properly ſtampt for inrolment, the officer will refuſe to inrol it; yet if he ſhould have recorded it, I know of no proviſion in any act relative to the ſubject, which invalidates the deed, after it hath been once recorded, or that makes the deficiency of ſtamps prevent its becoming a record of the court.. For ſtamps are impoſed by acts of parliament; nothing therefore relative thereunto can alter the common law, but by expreſs words. (*a*) "Statutes are not preſumed to make any alteration "in the common law, further or otherwiſe, than "the act does expreſsly declare." The nature of the deed remains, as it was at common law, which was paramount and independant of the duty upon ſtamps.

(*a*) 11 Mod. 150.

Upon full and mature consideration of this subject, I cannot help concluding my opinion, that if a judge do sign a *fiat* for the inrolment of a bargain and sale, which is required to be inrolled by the act of Henry VIII. and it be ingrossed upon proper stamps; and after that, it be recorded in the court, it hath answered the intent of the statute, which requires it to be inrolled. When I say thus much, I am also of opinion that in no case a judge should ever sign a *fiat* for inrolment, without the acknowledgment of that party to the deed, whose execution of it gives it efficacy and effect. (*a*) In the case of *Absolom* and *Anderton*, the acknowledgment was by the bargainors, viz. the masters and chaplains of the Savoy, before a master in Chancery, who went down for the purpose to their chapter house: so that if the parties had been common persons, every thing was perfectly right; but it being the case of a body corporate, who cannot do solemn acts by parole, nor otherwise than under their common seal; a question arose upon the validity of the inrolment. And it was agreed, *that the indenture being once inrolled, it was not material by what means, but was good being done.*

When it is considered, that the copy of any inrolment may be read in evidence, and that a deed ought not to be inrolled without the acknowledgment of a party to it, and that an acknowledgment binds the acknowledging party, and all claiming under him; when we also reflect that an acknowledgment of a deed, is but an avowal by the party, that the deed to be inrolled is his own act and deed, and that it is his wish and desire, that it be rendered notorious and perpetuated; I flatter myself, that it will be the conclusion of all my readers, that the inventions and devises of introducing nominal par-

(*a*) 3 Lev. 84.

ties to acknowledge deeds, and ſigning *fiats* for their inrolment, are but evaſions or perverſions of the real intent and purpoſe of inrolling deeds; and that conſequently therefore, one fixt, conſiſtent and effectual mode of inrolling deeds by the acknowledgment of the granting or operating party to the deed, ought to be eſtabliſhed, as it is provided for in the draft of the bill annexed hereunto.

Nothing can ſo ſolidly confirm the doctrine I have attempted to eſtabliſh, as to conſider the effects produced by the inrolment. For it hath been holden, (*a*) that until the deed be inrolled, the eſtate and freehold is in the bargainor, and nothing paſſes from him. So in *Billingham*'s caſe; " bargainee before inrolment, bargains and ſells to " another, and afterwards the firſt deed is inrolled, " and after that the ſecond: yet held, that nothing " paſſed, for he had not any eſtate in him at the " time of the bargain and ſale to give to a ſtran-" ger." As therefore the transfer of the land is the act of the bargainor, and the acknowledgment and inrolment of the indenture is but the continuation and completion of that act of transfer, it certainly ought to be done by the bargainor. And for this obvious reaſon was it ſaid by *Dyer*, that a bargainor is eſtopped by the inrolment from pleading either nonage or dureſs, or any matter, which diſproves the deed and deſtroys it.

## *Of the Inrolment of Wills.*

Whatever objections might be raiſed againſt inrolling every *deed* affecting land; yet confident I am, that the reaſons, which I am about to adduce, will prove the indiſpenſible neceſſity of inrolling all wills and deviſes of land, in order to render them

(*a*) Moore 42.

notorious, public, perpetual and authentic. It is no ſmall ſatisfaction to find my opinion ſupported by ſo great a man as Sir Matthew Hal.. (*a*) "It were well, if ſome greater ſolemnity were re-"quired by law in wills, whereby lands are de-"viſed: for ever ſince the ſtatute of 34 Hen. 8. "more queſtions, not only of law, touching the "conſtructions of wills, but alſo of facts, ariſe, "than in any five general titles or concerns of lands "beſides." To ſee and perfectly comprehend the law, nothing is ſo effectual, as to trace it to its origin: to acquire an intuitive knowledge of an effect, we ſhould not be ignorant of the cauſe.

The power, which individuals in this country have been permitted to enjoy, of diſpoſing of their poſſeſſions even after death, ſeems *always* to have extended without interruption to perſonal property: ſuch as is money, goods, chattels, &c. but as to land, although the like power exiſted, and was exerciſed by our Saxon anceſtors, yet from the Norman conqueſt, to the days of Henry VIII. this power had ceaſed or run into deſuetude, and exiſted no longer, but by private cuſtom in ſome manors, boroughs and corporations.

The inconveniency of lands not being deviſeable was at length felt in a commercial country; and by the 32d Hen. VIII. c. 1. every one was enabled to deviſe all his lands holden in ſoccage, and two third parts of his lands holden by knights ſervice: and by 12 Car. II. c. 35. ſec. 1. all tenures are turned into free and common ſoccage; ſo that at preſent all lands whatſoever are deviſeable by ſtatute.

Notwithſtanding this act of Henry VIII. enabling individuals to deviſe their lands in the manner before mentioned; we find that in the days of Car. II.

(*a*) The before-mentioned pamphlet upon a general regiſtry.

when

when after the then late revolution and troubles, the nation began to enjoy peace and quiet, and commanded ſome cool leiſure to look forwards towards quieting and ſettling their titles to their poſſeſſions, (for at that time almoſt every man ſtood in abſolute need of it); they paſſed, *an act for the prevention of frauds and perjuries*, commonly called the ſtatute of frauds: (*a*) and amongſt other remedies adminiſtered by that act, was that of adding " greater " ſolemnity and notoriety to the publication of all " deviſes and bequeſts of any lands or tenements, " deviſeable either by force of the ſtatute of wills, " or by this ſtatute, or by force of the cuſtom of " Kent or the cuſtom of any borough or any other " particular cuſtom, which (from the 24th June " 1676) it was enacted, ſhould be in writing, " and ſigned by the party ſo deviſing the ſame, or " by ſome other perſon in his preſence, or by his " expreſs directions, and ſhould be atteſted and " ſubſcribed in the preſence of, and by his expreſs " direction, and ſhould be atteſted and ſubſcribed " in the preſence of the ſaid deviſor by three or " four credible witneſſes, or elſe they ſhould be " utterly void and of none effect." And the act provided alſo for the ſame degree of notoriety and publicity in cancelling, altering and revoking ſuch deviſes and bequeſts; and for the *amendment of the law in that particular*, enacted; that from thenceforth, " any eſtate *pour auter vie* ſhould be deviſe- " able by a will in writing, ſigned by the party ſo " deviſing the ſame, or by ſome other perſon in his " preſence, and by his expreſs directions atteſted " and ſubſcribed in the preſence of the deviſor, by " three or more witneſſes," &c.

Whoever reflects one moment upon theſe par-

(*a*) 29 Car. 2. c. 3.

liamentary

liamentary provisions for the additional solemnity and publicity of landed devises, more than in wills of personal property, cannot hesitate to conclude, that there is more reason also for such wills being perpetuated and preserved open to inspection, than the wills of personal property. A will moreover, by which land is devised, forms the most material part of the title to the land devised; and in every alienation or charge or settlement of it, it will ever be proper to trace and prove the title, at least for sixty years back. Nothing of this, is applicable to the bequest of personal goods and chattels.

### *Of the Spiritual or Ecclesiastical Courts.*

It is foreign from my purpose to trace and account for the introduction of any legal jurisdiction or tribunal into this country, which is not governed and regulated by the municipal law of the land. For in fact, the civil law (by which is meant the Roman or Justinian code) is as foreign and distinct from the municipal law of this country, as the Talmud or the Coran.

At a time, when the clergy had monopolized all literature and knowledge, it was an easy matter for them to extend that superiority, together with what their spiritual character and functions gave them, over generations more docile in faith and pliant to credulity, than the present, to a dominion, sway or influence over the temporalties of their flocks. From the right, which the ordinaries acquired to distribute and apply the personal goods of intestates *pro salute animarum defunctorum* according to the doctrine of those days, that the persons, who had the charge and care of men's souls in their lifetime, were the most proper to see to the application of their property after death, many abuses gradually crept into this authority and power.

Such ever has been, and ſuch ever will be the caſe, where the ſpiritual power aſſumes, or even receives any temporal juriſdiction. For if any ſpiritual authority does exiſt, it is in its nature eſſentially diſtinct from and independant of all human inſtitution: and from the inſtant, that it raiſes itſelf upon any other baſis, than that of the divine gift or miſſion, it perverts its origin and inſtitution, and becomes of courſe much more liable, from an heterogeneous principle, to all ſorts of abuſes, than if it were a mere temporal power or juriſdiction.

### *How the Right of Adminiſtration probably came to the Ordinary.*

It is no uncommon thing at the cloſe of life, that a perſon repenting of his ſins, may from a juſt principle of reſtitution or reparation, wiſh to have a certain ſum of money applied in a ſecret manner, in order to avoid ſcandal or diſgrace; and in thoſe countries, where auricular confeſſion is in uſe (as it then was in England) ſuch applications are uſually left to be made by the ſpiritual director of the penitent, who may probably have ſuggeſted the propriety, or inſiſted upon the neceſſity of them. It is alſo frequent (amongſt thoſe, who hold, that there is in the next life a place of temporary puniſhment, where we are purified from our ſlighter failings, which have not deſerved the eternal torments of hell, and that the prayérs and interceſſions of the living are an inducement to the mercy of Almighty God, to alleviate and abbreviate their pains and puniſhments) to make donations to particular churches and particular perſons, in order that certain ſacrifices and prayers may be offered up to Almighty God with this view, for the repoſe of their

ſouls:

ſouls: as we read in the books of the Maccabees (*a*). "He making a gathering ſent 12000 "drachms of ſilver to Jeruſalem, to have ſacrifice "offered for the ſins of the dead, well and right-"eouſly thinking of the reſurrection: for unleſs "he hoped, that they who were ſlain, ſhould riſe "again, it would ſeem ſuperfluous and vain to "pray for the dead. It is therefore a holy and "healthful cogitation to pray for the dead, that "they may be looſed from their ſins." Thus as in thoſe days, (viz. 200 years before the coming of Chriſt) the money, which was thought proper to be applied to this purpoſe, was ſent to the prieſts of the temple, ſo probably was it, in latter times, depoſited in like manner with the prieſts of the new law: and ſo by degrees, not only that part of the property of the deceaſed, which was devoted to theſe purpoſes, was often veſted in the ordinary, but the whole perſonal eſtate became veſted in him, with an expreſſed or implied injunction and obligation of applying the reſidue or remainder (if any) unto or amongſt the relations of the deceaſed. This appears to me to have been the original ſpirit and intention of the ordinary's power in this reſpect. But a mixture of ſpiritual and temporal power will never blend properly together.

It is very evident, that abuſes of this right and power crept in at a very early period: for in the year 1285 (*b*) the legiſlature takes notice, that "whereas after the death of a perſon dying in-"teſtate and in debt to ſeveral, *the goods come to* "*the ordinary to be diſpoſed* (behold here the uſage,

(*a*) 2 Mac. XII. 43. Although theſe books are holden to be apocrypha, yet they are read in the church of England *for example of life and inſtruction of manners* (Art. IV.) which would not be, if they did not contain true and authentic hiſtory.

(*b*) 13 Ed. 1. c. 19.

into which the abuſe had crept, and then follows the remedy) " the ordinary from henceforth ſhall " be bound to anſwer the debts, as far forth as the " goods of the dead will extend, in the ſame man- " ner as his executors would have been bounden, " if he had made a will."

### *The Spiritual Courts had not the original Cognizance of Wills.*

By the ancient Britiſh laws, the probate and juriſdiction of wills did originally (as it always ought) belong to the temporal courts: for we find in Glanvill, the earlieſt writer and moſt authentic quoter of the common law (*a*), that there is a *writ*, which lies at common law, to recover a legacy. And in the regiſter there appears to be a writ *de rationabili parte*. It was about the time of Richard the 3d, that wills were proved in the ſpiritual courts (*b*). In all other nations they are proved in the temporal courts. And in many places in England, even at this day, the lords of manors have the probate of wills (*c*): and Tremayle, who was then king's ſerjeant, told the Court, that he was ſteward of ſeveral manors in his county, where both freehold and copyhold tenants proved their wills before him in the courts baron; which particular cuſtoms were (as before obſerved) a retention or relict of the ancient general law or uſage. Linwood, who was dean of the Arches, and wrote about the time of Hen. VI. doth confeſs, that the probate of wills did belong to the ordinaries, *non de communi jure*, but by cuſtom. And archbiſhop Parker publiſhed a book in 1573, in which he ſays

(*a*) Lib. 6. c. 6, 7.
(*b*) Fitz. Teſtam. 4.
(*c*) Nelſon lex Teſtamentaria, p. 462. Henſloe's caſe, 9 Rep. 38.

nec

*nec ullam habebant episcopi authoritatem, præter eam quam a rege acceptam referebant; testamenta probandi authoritatem non habebant, nec administrationis potestatem cuique delegare non poterant* (*a*).

Anciently (*b*), upon the death of an intestate, the son was intitled to have the heriots due to him, which were appointed by law, that by the lord's advice or judgment *the intestate's goods be divided amongst his wife and children and the next of kin, according as to every one of them of right belongs.* And it appears clearly conclusive from the words of the laws of Edw. the Confessor, that the ordinary in those days, had nothing to do with the administration or distribution of goods of the intestate (*c*). *Habeant hæredes ejus pecuniam et terram ejus sine aliquâ diminutione, et rectè dividant inter se*; for if this right of the heir to the goods and land had not been under the usual temporal jurisdiction of the common law, it would certainly have been mentioned to be under some other jurisdiction. And Mr. Selden says expresly, " that " until King John's time, it seems the jurisdic- " tion over the intestate's goods, was as of other " inheritances also, in the temporal courts; yet no " sufficient testimony is found to prove it expresly: " only when the common laws of those times speak " of intestates, they determined the succession by " like division, as those of the Saxon times. In " certain laws attributed to Will. the First (*d*), " we read, *Si home moruust sans devise, si departent* " *les infants, leritè inter se per ovell.* And after, in " Henry I. laws (*e*), *Si quis baronum vel hominum*

(*a*) Lambert, fol. 167. Selden, fol. 184.

(*b*) Canut. leg. c. 68, & Selden of the disposition or administration of intestates goods, p. 15.

(*c*) Leg. Ed. Conf. cap. de Heretoch. of Croland.

(*d*) MS. in the Cotton lib. attributed to Ingulph.

(*e*) Matthew Paris.

" *meorum præventus, vel armis vel infirmitate, pecu-*
" *niam suam nec aederit, nec dare disposuerit, uxor*
" *sua sive liberi aut parentes et legitimi homines sui*
" *pro animâ ejus eam dividant, sicut eis melius visum*
" *fuerit.* Here is the first mention, as I remem-
" ber, of any thing occurring in our laws, or his-
" tories of the dispositions of the intestate's goods,
" *pro animâ ejus:* which indeed might have been
" fitly subjected to the view at least of the church.
" But no mention as yet of any ecclesiastical power,
" that tends that way; I rather think, that there-
" fore no use or practice was of administration
" committed, direction given, or meddling with
" the goods by the ordinaries: but all was by
" friends or kindred, *juxta consilium discretorum vi-*
" *rorum,* &c.

" Neither doth that of Glanvill, which was writ-
" ten under Henry II. tell us of any thing of the
" ordinaries power in this case, although it hath
" express mention of testaments, and the churches
" jurisdiction of them: indeed we there find (*a*) that
" if no executor be named, then *possunt propinqui*
" *et consanguinei testatoris* take upon them the
" executorship, and sue in the king's court against
" such, as hinder the due payment of legacies,
" which also agrees well enough with that before
" cited out of the laws of Henry I."

The first interference of the church, in the application of the goods of intestates, that I can trace, is in the charter granted or made by King John in the 17th year of his reign, at Runnymead (*b*): *Si quis liber homo intestatus decesserit, catalla sua per manus propinquorum parentum et amicorum suorum per visum ecclesiæ distribuantur, salvis*

(*a*) Glanv. lib. 7. cap. 6.

(*b*) In a MS. preserved by Matt. Par. Roger of Wendover, and Tho. Rudman.

*uni*

*uni cuique debitis, quæ defunctus eis debebat.* These words *per visum ecclesiæ* cannot in any manner import a judicial or any other power in the church: they seem to import a sort of testimony, or notoriety only of its being done in the face of the church, or before the ordinary, as it is said in writs of summons *per visum proborum legalium hominum,* or as Mr. Selden understands it, *by the direction and advice of the ordinary.*

We are to observe, that by this charter the administration and distribution of the goods of the intestate were directed to be made only by the next of kin and the friends of the deceased, *per manus propinquorum parentum et amicorum suorum*: and yet very soon afterwards we may trace the interference of the ordinaries gaining gradual ground towards that absolute dominion, power and authority, which they afterwards exercised without controul. For we read in Bracton, who was a judge in the reign of Henry 3d (*a*), " *Si liber homo intestatus et subitò* " *decesserit, dominus suus nil intromittat de bonis de-* " *functi, nisi de hoc tantum quod ad ipsum pertinuerit* " *(scilicet quod habeat suum heriott) sed ad ecclesiam* " *et amicos pertinebit executio bonorum.*"

The ordinaries, soon after they had acquired this joint power with the next of kin, soon found means to exclude the latter from any participation whatsoever in the administration and distribution of the goods of intestates: for in the 42d year of the reign of the said King Henry the 3d, we read of an article granted in the synod of London (*b*): " *Idem* " *quod mortuo laico sine testamento, non capiantur* " *bona ipsius in manus dominorum. Sed inde solvan-* " *tur debita ipsius, et residua in usûs filiorum, servo-*

(*a*) Bracton, lib. 2. de acq. rer. dom. c. 26, sect. 2.
(*b*) In annal. Bartomensis con. pernes. V. cl. Thorm. Allen Oxon. MS. A. 1257.

"*rum et proximorum indigentium, pro ſalute animæ*
"*defuncti, in pios uſûs per ordinarios committantur,*
"*niſi quatenùs fuerit domino ſuo obligatus.*" It is curious to obſerve the gradation of this uſurped or acquired power of the ordinaries; firſt, as we have ſeen, they were called in as witneſſes or conſulted as adviſers; then they became joint executors or adminiſtrators; then ſole adminiſtrators and diſtributors of the goods of the inteſtates: but ſtill the *pious uſes*, to which they pretended to apply them, were the payment of debts and the ſuccour and relief of the children and needy relations of the deceaſed. Nor did the abuſes of this uſurped power ceaſe, till the ordinaries had acquired an arbitrary and diſcretionary right or authority of diſtributing and diſpoſing of all the goods of the inteſtates. The different gradations of this uſurped power are the cleareſt proofs of its introduction and eſtabliſhment, upon the decline and abolition of the ancient laws and cuſtoms of the realm.

*Lands were formerly deviſeable.*

It appears both from records and hiſtory, that in the days of our Saxon anceſtors, goods (or perſonal eſtate) as well as lands paſſed by deſcent; and the lord of the fee was in the place of a judge, to ſee upon the death of any of his tenants, that there ſhould be an equality in the diſtribution, as well of the goods, as of the lands amongſt the children and next of kin: for if there were children, they excluded all the kindred of a more remote degree, and therefore the rule was, *Si liberi non ſunt, proximus gradus in poſſeſſione fratres, patrui, avunculi*, &c.

The cuſtom of Gavel Kind, which was retained all through Kent, and ſubſiſts even to this day in ſome parts of that county, is nothing more, than a relict

relict of the ancient common law, according to that, *Si quis inteſtatus obierit, liberi ejus hæreditatem æqualiter dividant* (*a*).

This alſo clearly proves the ancient law of deviſing land; for inteſtacy is not ſpoken of, where there is not a cuſtom or uſage of willing.

### *The Norman Feudal Syſtem incompatible with the Power of deviſing Lands*, &c.

When William the Norman found it political to change the landed tenures of the kingdom, and introduce a more rigorous form or mode of the feudal ſyſtem, it annihilated at once the power of deviſing lands; for a feud was at firſt no more, than a right, which the vaſſal had to take the profits of his lord's lands, rendering unto him ſuch feudal duties and ſervices, as belong to military tenure; ſo that the tenant had only the uſe of the land, and the property ſtill continued in the lord. Theſe feuds were originally holden only at the will of the lord, but afterwards were continued to the tenant during his life; in either of which caſes, they could not be diſpoſed of by will, for a will is the actual diſpoſition of a right or intereſt, which ſurvives the teſtator. Feuds, in proceſs of time, became hereditary and perpetual, and even then the perſonal ſervices and duties, which the feudal tenant was bound to pay to his lord, were of ſuch a nature, as eſſentially precluded the power of diſpoſing of the feud by will; for there were certain profits of *ward* and *marriage*, which became due to the lord, if the heir was under age, at the death of the tenant; and if of full age, the land fell into the lord, who became entitled to *relief*; the payment of which *relief* was in the nature of a new purchaſe,

(*a*) Lambert fo. 167, & Selden fo. 184.

or a price paid to the lord for the land. The feudal tenants were bound moreover to the defence of their lord's perſon in the field, and to attend and give him their advice and counſel once at leaſt in three weeks in his courts. Strength of body and ability of mind were therefore requiſite, to render theſe ſervices properly and duly to the lord. And in this ſyſtem, it certainly was reaſonable, that the lord ſhould have the education of the heir, that he might inſtruct, educate and form him ſo, as to be capable of rendering the due ſervices of the feud to the lord. It was therefore incompatible with the feudal principle, that any man ſhould be empowered by will to diſinherit the heir, and ſo preclude the lord from his beneficial chances of *ward*, *marriage* and *relief*, and deprive him by an impotent ſubſtitute of the civil and military ſervices, to which by tenure he was entitled. Beſides, (ſays Baron Gilbert), (*a*) " this way of conveyance " wanted that ſolemnity, which the feudiſts thought " neceſſary to eſtabliſh in transferring lands; and " if at any time a diſpute ſhould ariſe, it might " be the eaſier determined by the *pares comitatus*, " who were witneſſes to that notorious and public " manner of conveying by livery; and, for that " reaſon, I believe copyhold land was taken to be " out of the ſtatute of 32d Henry VIII. For their " ſurrender which is required, as well in deviſes as " in other alienations, anſwers the notoriety of livery and ſeiſin, and conſequently out of the reaſons of the prohibition of the feudal law. Thus " the law continued till the invention of uſes, " which were firſt found out by the clergy, to " evade the ſtatutes of mortmain." We have already ſaid ſo much of the 32d of Henry VIII. that it will be unneceſſary to ſay more of it at preſent.

(*a*) Gilbert's Law of Deviſes, p. 9.

Of

## *Of the different Modes of inrolling Deeds in the different Courts.*

Although I have made extensive searches amongst the records of the different courts, yet I do not claim the pretension of having searched so minutely, as to give a strict and accurate account of every deed there recorded; the result of my searches has however more and more convinced me of the necessity of a regular and uniform mode of issuing warrants for inrolling deeds and wills. By considering minutely the different sorts of warrants, by virtue of which, deeds and wills are now usually entered upon the rolls, and thereby become recorded in court, we shall be enabled to judge and determine, what sort of warrants ought only to be issued for that purpose.

We have before considered the original intent and meaning of a party acknowledging a deed, and the effects produced by that acknowledgment; and I appeal to the judgment of those, who have really considered them, whether any other method besides that of acknowledgment, can by possibility answer the ends, for which deeds are inrolled. The inrolling act of Henry VIII. is compulsive upon all persons, who grant land by bargain and sale for a pecuniary consideration. The inrolling act of Geo. I. is compulsive upon all Catholics, who affect their lands by deed or will. The time limited by both acts for inrolling such deeds, is six lunar months from their date or delivery. Upon their inrolment or non-inrolment within that space of time, absolutely depends their validity or nullity. And according to every idea of common sense and plain reason, the act, by which the deed acquires its validity, and the omission, by which it becomes a nullity, ought to rest with that party to the deed, whoſe execution of it gives it effect; and upon this principle, it is generally ſaid, that the grantor ſhould always acknowledge the deed. Nothing can more plainly ſpeak this general preſumption or opinion, than the proviſions in the aforeſaid regiſtering acts, for the inrolment of bargains and ſales in the regiſtry of the reſpective riding of the county of York, where the lands compriſed in the deed lie. Theſe acts require, as a previous requiſite to the inrolment of any ſuch deed, that the grantor ſhall acknowledge it before two juſtices of the peace of that riding; preſuming, that if the deed had been inrolled in a court of record, it would have been acknowledged before one of the judges of the court by the grantor, as, in my humble opinion, it ought to be. For I again repeat my opinion, that no deed whatſoever ought to be inrolled, till it has been acknowledged by the party, whoſe execution of it gives its effect, before ſuch authority, as can thereupon iſſue a warrant to the officers of the court to inrol it.

I have before ſaid much of the nature of *fiats*, under which many of the Roman catholic deeds are inrolled. But then this ſort of warrant ſeems to have been generally confined to ſuch deeds, unleſs in ſome few inſtances they have been iſſued for inrolling deeds *pro ſalvâ cuſtodiâ*. It ſhould appear *ex vi termini*, that deeds ſo inrolled were kept or depoſited in ſome cuſtody, which is not the caſe. And yet it is ſaid in Salkeld, (*a*) that "*at common law*," there was "an inrolment *pro* "*ſalva cuſtodiâ*;" and it appears from what I have ſaid before, viz. that, as the court would not admit of a voluntary inrolment, without the acknowledgment of the party, much leſs would they inrol a deed under a coercive ſtatute without it; and

(*a*) Salk. 348.

therefore

therefore, when ſuch voluntary inrolments were made, the deeds were uſually acknowledged previouſly by the party. It often happens, that perſons wiſhing to ſecure and perpetuate the memory of deeds, after the parties to them are dead, have applied to the judges of the court for a warrant to the officer to inrol them; and after the deaths of the parties, (as in wills) what other warrant can be iſſued than a *fiat*? And it may be fairly preſumed, that wherever a *fiat* has been iſſued for inrolling ſuch a deed, when the granting or operating party to it was living, it has been the preſumption and ſuppoſition of the judge, who ſigned the *fiat*, that the party was dead, or otherwiſe, that he would have come to acknowledge his own act and deed, if he wiſhed it to be inrolled and recorded.

From the effects produced by the inrolment of a deed, it muſt be allowed, that there is a very material difference between a deed inrolled, and a deed not inrolled; and it would be highly unreaſonable, that this difference ſhould be made to depend upon the act of an utter ſtranger to the deed: for either the *fiat* is ſigned by the judge, without any queſtion or examination into the reaſon, motive or pretenſions of the perſon, who preſents the warrant for ſigning; or it is ſigned upon the affidavit of an atteſting witneſs to the ſealing and delivery of the deed, by one of the parties to it. In both theſe caſes, the deed may come to be recorded in court, without the intention, and even againſt the wiſh of the grantor; and if we reflect, that the inrolment is but the completion of the act of tranſfer, as was before obſerved, the abſurdity of its being completed without the privity or againſt the wiſh of the grantor, will appear in its true colours.

The court of Chancery very frequently, and the court of King's Bench in ſome inſtances, has adopted another method of inrolling bargains and ſales, viz. by by the affidavit of an attesting witness to the execution of the deed; and although I cannot even invent a solid and substantial reason for their so doing, yet must it be allowed, that they have the sanction of authority for it; and so much cannot be said in favour of *fiats*. It is said (*a*) "*that a* "*deed may be inrolled without the examination of the* "*party, upon proof by witnesses, that the party de-* "*livered it.*" And (*b*) "*party died before acknow-* "*ledgment, yet the deed was inrolled.*"

To reduce this subject to some consistent degree of reason and regularity, we must allow, that no deed whatsoever should be inrolled, without the acknowledgment of the granting or efficient party to the deed, if he be living; and as it may often happen, that not only by death, but even by sickness, business and inconveniency, a person may be prevented or hindred from appearing personally before a judge or magistrates, to acknowledge a deed; yet may he always at the same time execute a special warrant of attorney, which should be annexed unto or indorsed upon, or even included in the deed, to empower some proper person to acknowledge the execution of it on his or her behalf, before a judge or magistrates, and to desire that it may be inrolled in a proper court. Such a practice is not only warrantable upon the general principle of all powers of attorney, *qui facit per alium, facit per se*; but also more especially upon another axiom, that *qui potest majus, potest & minus*. For if a person can legally depute another to seal and deliver a deed for him, he certainly may empower him to acknowledge his own execution. But this is a matter so plain and simple, that I shall neither quote authorities, nor say any thing more upon the subject.

(*a*) Godb. 270. (*b*) 3 Leon 84.

Points

Points of practice are often the ſtrongeſt evidence of points of law; and nothing more forcibly proves, that the law intended, and in fact preſumes, that all deeds inrolled are or ought to be acknowledged, than the titles, which are prefixed to the inrolments of each term, in every one of the four different courts of record; which invariably run, *cognita et irrotulata*, that is acknowledged and inrolled, &c. whence it is a juſt inference, that none, but ſuch as are acknowledged, are ſuppoſed to be inrolled.

## *The Objections againſt the Notoriety of Deeds and Wills affecting Lands.*

The grand, and indeed the only objection, which ever hath been raiſed againſt the notoriety of deeds and wills affecting lands is, that thereby family ſecrets and tranſactions may be laid open and divulged; but this will ſoon vaniſh, when we reflect, that every will of perſonal property muſt be proved in the ſpiritual court; under the ſeal of which, letters teſtamentary are granted, by which the executor is enabled to maintain an action; and that a will once proved, is depoſited as a public and notorious act of the party, to which all perſons, but more eſpecially the next of kin (who in caſe of an inteſtacy would have been intitled to the perſonal eſtate of the deceaſed) may have recourſe, and know without being driven to the expence and trouble of a ſuit or action, upon what ground, and in what manner they are deprived of thoſe rights, which the law would have caſt upon them, if the deceaſed had not counteracted its effects by a will. I have never known any inconveniency ariſe from ſuch publication and notoriety of wills: on the contrary, I believe there are few perſons, who have ever been concerned in the wills

of

of their relations or friends, who have not reaſon to rejoice and approve of their being thus regularly depoſited, and open to public inſpection.

If then in the bequeſt of perſonal goods and chattels, the title to which is ever more ſimple and obvious than to land, this notoriety is required by law, how much more requiſite is it, when an heir at law is either wholly or partially diſinherited, or made liable and ſubjected to a temporary or permanent incumbrance, or is crampt and limited in his inheritance, that the inſtrument ſhould be publiſhed and recorded, ſo as to be open to public inſpection and conſideration, without action at law or ſuit in equity! For it is undeniable, that all muniments and titles to land, and emphatically ſuch as go to interrupt the legal courſe of inheritance, ſhould be matters of publicity, notoriety and perpetuity.

As the power of deviſing lands, guardianſhips, &c. was either given or received by ſtatute, the wills, by which they are deviſed, are not ſubjected to the ſpiritual court, in *which alone* a public entry of wills is made. (*a*) Where "a guardianſhip "of a child is deviſed by will, it ſhall not be "proved in the ſpiritual court, becauſe it being "a power given by the ſtatute, it properly belongs "to the courts at Weſtminſter to determine, whe-"ther the deviſe was made purſuant to the ſtatute, "and therefore like wills, by which lands are de-"viſed, it is uſually proved by witneſſes in Chan-"cery." But ſuch probate in Chancery is not compulſory; it is no copy, and therefore no record of the will; nor does it operate any other effect, than the perpetuation of the teſtimony of the witneſſes to the execution of the will by the deviſor. It rarely happens, that deviſes of land are made by

(*a*) 1 Vent. 207.

wills,

wills, which do not diſpoſe of ſome perſonal eſtate: the quere then ariſes, when the land deviſed is the principal object of the teſtament, ſhall it, or ſhall it not be adjudged by the ſpiritual court? Now what can be more abſurd and inconſiſtent, than, that an inſtrument, by which property is diſpoſed of in this country, ſhall be liable to a deciſion by two ſeparate, diſtinct and contrary laws? For ſuch in fact are the Roman law, by which the eccleſiaſtical courts judge; and the Engliſh law, which determines the deciſions of our courts of law and equity. (*a*) Libel in the ſpiritual court, "to prove "a will, the defendant ſuggeſted for a prohibi-"tion, that in the will there were lands and lega-"cies deviſed, and that the teſtator was *non com-*"*pos mentis*; but the prohibition was denied, be-"cauſe the ſtatute of Hen. VIII. never intended "to diminiſh the juriſdiction of the ſpiritual court, "as to probates; and it might be very inconve-"nient to ſtay the probate in this caſe, becauſe "whilſt it is ſtayed, the executor cannot ſue for "debts; and by that means they may be loſt, and "the will not performed; and it would be to no "purpoſe to grant a prohibition as to the lands, "becauſe as to them the probate is *coram non ju-*"*dice*, and cannot be given in evidence in any "court of law."

Who does not ſee the extremity of folly, in obliging deviſees in general to enter and prove wills paſſing lands in a court, which hath not, nor can have any cognizance or juriſdiction over them. Independant of the uſeleſs expence, it is highly derogatory from the dignity and reſpect due to our national juriſprudence. (*b*) "Where a will "is made of lands and goods, the temporal courts

(*a*) Partridge v. Cave, 2 Salk. 553.
(*b*) Netter v. Brett, W. Jones 355. Cr. Car. 391. 395.

" will not prohibit it to be proved in the ſpiritual " court. 'Tis true, this was againſt the opinion of " Juſtice Croke, becauſe the land being the prin- " cipal, the ſpiritual court had no authority in ſuch " caſe. And that it would be inconvenient if they " ſhould; for the ſentence given in that court " might have ſome influence upon any ſuit, which " might happen in the temporal courts concerning " the land. (*a*) And it is ſaid elſewhere, that a " will of lands ought not to be proved in the ſpi- " ritual court." From thence and the like caſes, we ſee the inconveniency and incongruity of the preſent law of deviſes of lands, and the urgent neceſſity of publiſhing and perpetuating all wills and codicils in any manner affecting them; for by them, titles are weakened or confirmed, heirs at law diſinherited, purchaſers and mortgagees ſtrengthened or ſhaken in their purchaſes or ſecurities, and all perſons claiming right under the deviſor, moſt materially affected. Every end of notoriety and perpetuity will be anſwered by inrolling wills affecting lands, in the like manner, as wills of perſonalty are now entered for weaker reaſons, in the ſpiritual court. As the law ever favours the heir, it will preſume *him* to have the right, until it be proved that he is diſinherited: he ought not therefore upon any principle of law or equity to be driven to expence and litigation, in order to prove his own diſheriſon; eſpecially as ſuch diſheriſon is effected by a legal act or inſtrument, which is warranted by an expreſs ſtatute. But yet the title, which is acquired under ſuch will, is in its nature inferior to the title acquired by the deſcent, which is caſt at law. (*b*) " So if a deviſe be made to John Stiles " and his heirs, who is heir at law to the deviſor,

(*a*) Hill v. Thornton 118.
(*b*) 3 Co. 31. a. Plowden's Com. 344. p.

" this

"this is a void deviſe; and the heir ſhall take by "deſcent as his better title, for the deſcent "ſtrengthens his title, by taking away the entry "of ſuch, as may poſſibly have right to the eſtate; "whereas if he claims by deviſe, he is in by pur-"chaſe."

It is a decided point (*a*), "that where a man "makes a general deviſe of all his lands, and af-"terwards purchaſes other lands without any new "publication of his will, and dies, the after-pur-"chaſed lands ſhall not paſs by the will, but ſhall "go to the heir at law; for the ſtatute impowers "only perſons *having* lands to deviſe, and he had "not theſe after purchaſed lands at the time of "making his will, and therefore not within the "ſtatute. Beſides ſince the intent of the deviſor "is the beſt rule for conſtruing wills, it will be "very reaſonable, that he never deſigned to con-"vey theſe particular lands, ſince he had them not "in his power nor poſſeſſion, when he ſettled "the diſpoſition of his other poſſeſſions." The ſtatute of Char. II. requires the atteſtation of three credible perſons to every will paſſing land: now is it not highly unreaſonable, that the heir at law, who is ſo materially intereſted in the date of the will, or any codicil that may amount to a re-publication of the will, and in the validity or nul-lity of a will, by reaſon of the requiſitions of the ſtatute of Char. II. ſhould be driven to his action to learn theſe ſimple points, upon which his own right hinges? So far from the deviſee's not being compelled to publiſh and manifeſt his title under the will, which is the caſe at preſent, I rather think he ought moreover to be obliged, within a ſhort limited time after the death of the teſtator, to ſerve the heir at law with an atteſted copy of the will.

(*a*) Gilbert. Law of Deviſes, p. 79.

I have ſaid thus much of the legal, equitable and political effects, that an univerſal inrolment of all deeds and wills affecting lands muſt neceſſarily produce: it remains incumbent upon me to account to the public in a ſatisfactory manner, for the innovations, changes and alterations, introduced into the draught of the bill, which I have planned for the intended purpoſe, and ſubjoined to theſe ſheets for the ſatisfaction of the public. I have choſen to be minute and particular in the draught, rather than propoſe the heads of a bill; judging, I hope rightly, that a more juſt and ſatisfactory judgment will be formed upon a plan executed, than executory.

It is a matter well known, that the erection and eſtabliſhment of county regiſters have been at different times ſuggeſted, propoſed and attempted in parliament, and always upon the principles, upon which I have endeavoured to ſhew the propriety and exigency of all deeds and wills affecting land being inrolled. It ſeems beyond queſtion, that the record of a deed ſhould not depend upon the experience, attention or judgment of the attorney or agent who records it, nor ſhould it be otherwiſe recorded for this reaſon, than *verbatim* from the original. We have before ſeen how extremely miſchievous the preſent method of entering the memorials of deeds is in the counties of York and Middleſex. I know not who E. B. Eſquire was, who publiſhed the beforementioned pamphlet in 1696: it is however ſatisfactory to find perſons coaleſce in opinion at the diſtance of a century, eſpecially when every reaſon for that opinion, hath been acquiring ground and ſtrength in a moſt rapid and accumulated degree during the whole intermediate time. For the truth of this obſervation I only appeal to the reflection of each of my readers. " It would make the title of freehold eſtates as

" certain

" certain as that of copyholds: of which there is " no certainty now, by reafon of latent deeds. " 2dly. It would prevent frauds in buying and fel- " ling, borrowing and lending. The borrower " could not impofe upon the lender, becaufe his " eftate would appear in the regifter, as it was; " nor could the lender impofe any hard terms up- " on the borrower, becaufe he would be able in a " fhort time to pay him off and transfer the debt " to another man. 3dly. This would certainly " lower the intereft of money, increafe trade and " hufbandry." And in fetting forth the inconve- niency and difficulties that he apprehended would be raifed againft this plan, he continues: " 1ft. This " will prevent great numbers of lawfuits, for which " there will then be no occafion, frequent fines for " procuration and continuation money, which will " bring great lofs to the lawyers and money-fcri- " veners, and to fome of the moft thriving ufu- " rers. 2dly. It will difcover thofe men, that have " mortgaged their lands two, three or more times " over, and perhaps for more than they are worth. " 3dly. It will reduce the greateft ufurer to " moderation and fair dealings. I do therefore ex- " pect that all thefe men will oppofe it to the ut- " moft, as it is their intereft to do; for though they " cannot take away the integrity of an honeft man, " yet great care is to be taken, it may not be " known which are fuch. For when knaves are " once detected, they are undone; and by them " the lawyer, money-fcrivener, &c. get all their " wealth."

DRAUGHT of a Bill for requiring the Inrolment of all Deeds, Wills, and Codicils relating to, touching or affecting any Freehold and Leasehold Lands, Tenements or Hereditaments within the kingdom of England and dominion of Wales, and for other purposes therein mentioned.

Preamble.

WHEREAS it is of the most important consequence to purchasers and lenders of money upon land security, that the titles of the vendors and borrowers of such money, should be so clearly known and ascertained, that no possible fraud nor deceit can be practised against *bonâ fide* purchasers, mortgagees or other incumbrancers, by reason of any preconveyance or secret prior debt, charge or incumbrance:

And whereas it is consistent with the principle of the ancient laws of this realm, that the most solemn notoriety and publication should attend every change and affection of lands, tenements and hereditaments:

And whereas parliament hath at different times found it expedient to enact, that all deeds and wills affecting lands in certain counties should be registered, and that certain other deeds and wills should be inrolled or registered throughout the nation:

And whereas the provisions contained in such several acts of parliament made for the inrolment or registering of deeds and wills, have

have by experience been found in many instances insufficient and inadequate to the ends and purposes intended to be effected by the said acts:

And whereas upon full consideration of the matter, it hath appeared reasonable and expedient to repeal all the aforesaid acts, and to make one general act for the inrolment of all deeds, wills and codicils, by which any freehold or leasehold lands, tenements or hereditaments throughout England and Wales, shall be in any manner affected:

Be it therefore declared and enacted by the King's most excellent Majesty, by and with the advice and consent of the lords spiritual and temporal and commons in parliament assembled, and by the authority of the same, that the statute made in the 27th year of the reign of 27 H. 8.
his late majesty King Henry VIII. "*for inrolling of bargains and sales*;" and also 5 Eliz.
an act made in the 5th year of the reign of her late majesty Queen Elizabeth, intituled, "*An act for the inrolment of indentures of bargains and sales in the queen's majesty's courts of the counties of Lancaster, Chester, and bishoprick of Durham*;" and also so much of an act made in the 21st year of 21 Jac. 1.
his late majesty King James the first, intituled, "*An act against such, as shall levy any fine, suffer any recovery, acknowledge any statute, bail or judgment, in the name of any other person or persons not being privy and consenting thereto*," as relates to the acknowledgment of deeds inrolled; and also an act made 4 & 5 W. & M.
in the 4th and 5th years of their late majesties King William and Queen Mary, intituled, "*An act to prevent fraud by clandestine mortgages*;" and also so much of an act 7 & 8 Wil. 3d.
passed

paſſed in the 7th and 8th years of his ſaid late majeſty King William III. intituled, "*An act* "*for the continuing ſeveral acts of parliament* "*therein mentioned*," as perpetuates two ſeveral acts, one made in the 4th & 5th years of the reign of their ſaid late majeſties King William and Queen Mary, and the other in the 6th & 7th years of the reign of their ſaid late majeſties, *for the better diſcovery of*
2d & 3d Ann. *judgments in the court of King's Bench*; and alſo an act made in the 2d & 3d years of the reign of her late majeſty Queen Ann, intituled, "*An act for the public regiſtering of all* "*deeds, conveyances and wills, that ſhall be* "*made of any honors, manors, lands, tene-* "*ments or hereditaments within the weſt-* "*riding of the county of York, after the nine*
5th Ann. "*and twentieth of September* 1704;" and alſo one other act made in the 5th year of the reign of her ſaid late majeſty Queen Ann, intituled, "*An act for the inrolment of bargains* "*and ſales within the weſt-riding of the county* "*of York, in the regiſter-office there lately* "*provided, and for making the ſaid regiſter*
6th Ann. "*more effectual*;" and alſo one other act made in the 6th year of the reign of her ſaid late majeſty Queen Ann, intituled, "*An act for the public regiſtering of all deeds,* "*conveyances, wills and other incumbrances,* "*which ſhall be made of, or that may affect any* "*honors, manors, lands, tenements or here-* "*ditaments within the eaſt-riding of the county* "*of York, or the town and county of Kingſton-* "*upon-Hull, after the nine and twentieth day* "*of September* 1708, *and for rendering the* "*regiſter in the weſt-riding more complete*;"
7th Ann. and alſo one other act made in the 7th year of the reign of her ſaid late majeſty Queen Ann,

Ann, intituled, "*An act for the public regis-*
"*tering of deeds, conveyances and wills, and*
"*other incumbrances, which shall be made of,*
"*or that may affect any honors, manors, lands,*
"*tenements or hereditaments within the county*
"*of Middlesex, after the 29th day of September*
"1709;" and also one other act made in the 1st year of the reign of his late majesty King George I. intituled, "*An act to oblige*
"*Papists to register their names and real es-*
"*tates*;" and also one other act made in the 3d year of the reign of his said late majesty King George I. intituled, "*An act for explaining an*
"*act passed the last session of parliament, intituled,*
"*An act to oblige Papists to register their names*
"*and real estates, and for enlarging the time*
"*of such registry, and for securing purchases*
"*made by Protestants*;" and also one other act made in the 8th year of the reign of his late majesty King George II. intituled, "*An act*
"*for the public registering of deeds, convey-*
"*ances, wills and other incumbrances, that shall*
"*be made of, or that may affect any honors,*
"*manors, lands, tenements or hereditaments*
"*within the north-riding of the county of*
"*York, after the 29th day of September* 1736;" and all the matters and things therein severally and respectively contained, shall be, and are hereby repealed, annulled and made void to all intents and purposes whatsoever.

1 Geo. 1.

3 Geo. 1.

8 Geo. 2.

Repealed.

And be it further declared and enacted by the authority aforesaid, That from and after the day of in the year of our Lord 1789, no deed, will nor codicil, by which any lands, tenements or hereditaments (except copyhold or customary lands) be the same freehold or leasehold, situate, lying and being within the kingdom of England

No deed, will, nor codicil affecting land to be valid, unless inrolled within six months,

land or dominion of Wales, ſhall or may be exchanged, altered, paſſed, charged, incumbered or affected in any manner whatſoever, ſhall be effectual, good or valid in law or equity, unleſs ſuch deed, will or codicil within ſix calendar months to be computed reſpectively from the day of the date of ſuch deed, or from the death of ſuch teſtator or teſtatrix, dying within the kingdom of Great Britain or dominion of Wales, or within the ſpace of three years to be computed reſpectively from the date of the deed, in caſe ſuch deed ſhall have been executed out of the kingdom of Great Britain or Ireland, or from the death of every ſuch reſpective teſtator or teſtatrix, dying upon or in any parts beyond the ſeas, ſhall be inrolled in ſome one of his Majeſty's four courts of record at Weſtminſter, or in the court or office hereby appointed and eſtabliſhed in each county, riding or diviſion, for the inrolment of all deeds, wills and codicils, relating to, touching, concerning or affecting lands, tenements or hereditaments, ſituate, lying and being within ſuch county, riding or diviſion reſpectively, in the manner and form hereby directed, appointed and required.

or 3 years, if the deed or will be executed without the kingdom.

The inrolment to be notice to all perſons.

And be it further declared and enacted by the authority aforeſaid, That the actual inrolment of every ſuch deed, will or codicil, ſhall, from and after the ſaid day of in the year of our Lord 1789, be, and be adjudged, deemed and taken to be and to have been from the time of ſuch actual inrolment, expreſs and legal notice of the eſtates, limitations, truſts, charges, powers, conditions, reſervations, reſtrictions and proviſoes created, limited, declared, made, expreſſed and contained by and in ſuch deeds, wills or or codicils reſpectively, to all ſubſequent purchaſers, mortgagees, and other incumbrancers, and to all other perſons whomſoever, any thing herein, or in any other ſtatute contained, or any law, uſage or cuſtom of this kingdom to the contrary thereof in any way notwithſtanding.

And be it further declared and enacted, by the authority aforeſaid, That before any ſuch deed ſhall be inrolled, it ſhall be acknowledged by the granting party or parties to the ſame, or by ſuch party or parties thereto, whoſe execution thereof gives effect to ſuch deed, before any one of his Majeſty's juſtices of any of the courts of record, in which the ſame is intended to be inrolled, or before any maſter ordinary or extraordinary of the high court of Chancery, or before two juſtices of the peace for the county, riding or diviſion, in the court or office of which, ſuch deed is intended to be inrolled, and the name of ſuch judge, maſter in Chancery, or of ſuch juſtices of the peace, ſhall be ſubſcribed to ſuch acknowledgment; and the ſubſcription of the name or names of ſuch judge, maſter in Chancery, or juſtices of the peace, under ſuch acknowledgment, upon the face of the deed ſhall be the authority and warrant to the clerks, officers or commiſſioners of the reſpective courts or offices to inrol the ſame, who in caſe the deed, upon which ſuch acknowledgment ſhall appear to be ſubſcribed as aforeſaid, be properly ſtampt for inrolment, ſhall, and are hereby required to inrol the ſame according to the directions and requiſitions of this act: and the form of every ſuch acknowledgment to be written upon the face of every ſuch deed to be inrolled, ſhall be as followeth, that is to ſay:

Every deed to be inrolled ſhall be acknowledged before a judge, maſter in Chancery, or 2 juſtices of the peace.

" The

Form of acknowledgment.

"The execution of this deed having been
"acknowledged before me [or us] by
"A. B. the party [or and C. D. parties]
"thereto, who is [or are] bounden to ac-
"knowledge the ſame, let it be inrolled in
"his Majeſty's court of
"or in the court or office for inrolling
"deeds and wills in the county, [or
"riding] of this day of
"178 A. B. [or A. B. and C. D."]

Acknowledgments may be made by attornies.

Provided always, and be it further declared and enacted by the authority aforeſaid, That in caſe any ſuch perſon or perſons, who is or are hereby required to acknowledge every ſuch deed, before it ſhall be inrolled, ſhall not be able to appear perſonally before the judge, maſter in Chancery, or juſtices of the peace, in order to acknowledge and deſire the ſame to be inrolled in the proper court or office as aforeſaid, it ſhall and may be lawful to and for him, her or them, by ſome deed or deeds to be ſealed and delivered by him, her or them, in the preſence of, and to be atteſted by two or more credible witneſſes, to make, authorize and ordain one or more attorney or attornies for him, her or them, and in his, her or their name or names to acknowledge the execution of ſuch deed before ſuch judge, maſter in Chancery, or juſtice of the peace as aforeſaid, and for him, her or them to deſire, that ſuch deed may be inrolled: and every acknowledgment of ſuch party [or parties] to a deed ſo made by his, her or their attorney or attornies, for that purpoſe eſpecially made, authorized, and ordained as aforeſaid, ſhall be as effectual to all intents, conſtructions, and purpoſes whatſoever, as if the party or parties had perſonally appeared, and acknowledged

4 his,

his, her or their deed, before ſuch judge, maſter in Chancery, or juſtices of the peace as aforeſaid.

Provided always, and it is further declared and enacted by the authority aforeſaid, That whenever any perſon or perſons ſhall appear before ſuch judge, maſter in Chancery, or juſtices of the peace, to acknowledge a deed for and in the name or names of the party or parties to the deed, it ſhall and may be lawful to and for any ſuch judge, maſter in Chancery, or juſtices of the peace, whenever he or they ſhall think proper, to demand a proper legal affidavit of the execution of the warrant, power or letter of attorney by the party or parties hereby required to acknowledge the deed as aforeſaid, and to refuſe or withhold his or their ſignature to ſuch warrant or direction for inrolment, until ſuch affidavit as aforeſaid ſhall be produced: And the form of every ſuch acknowledgment to be written upon the face of every ſuch deed to be inrolled, where the party or parties cannot perſonally appear, ſhall be as follows, that is to ſay. Affidavit of the execution of the power of attorney may be acquired.

"The execution of this deed by A. B. the "party, [or and C. D. parties] who "is [or are] bounden to acknowledge "the ſame having been acknowledged "by E. F. [or and G. H.] lawfully con- "ſtituted the attorney [or attornies] for "the ſaid A. B. [or and C. D.] to acknow- "ledge and deſire the ſame to be inrolled "by virtue of a ſpecial and proper power "or warrant of attorney produced before "me [or us] for that purpoſe, let it be in- "rolled in his Majeſty's court of "or in the court or office for inrolling "deeds and wills in the county [or riding] "of Form of acknowledgment by attorney.

" of this day of 178

" A. B. [or A. B. and C. D.]"

And it is further declared and enacted by the authority aforesaid, That no executor nor executrix, nor other person or persons whosoever claiming or deriving any beneficial interest, right or advantage under any will or codicil, shall, from and after the day of in the year 1789, be enabled to sue for, claim or demand either at law or in equity, the whole or any part or parts of such beneficial interest, right or advantage, until the said will or codicil, in case it shall affect any freehold or leasehold lands, tenements or hereditaments, within the kingdom of England, or dominion of Wales, shall have been inrolled in manner aforesaid: And before any such will or codicil shall be inrolled, a fiat, warrant or direction for inrolment shall be written upon such will, upon a proper and legal affidavit being produced, or an oath being made of the execution of such will or codicil by the testator or testatrix by one or more of the subscribing witnesses thereto, before such judge, master in Chancery or justices of the peace, as aforesaid; and then such judge, master in Chancery, or justices of the peace, shall subscribe his or their name or names to such *fiat*, warrant or direction; the form whereof shall be as followeth:

Fiats for the inrolment of wills.

Form of the fiat.

" Upon the affidavit of A. B. being produced
" [or upon the oath of A. B. being made]
" before me [or us] of the legal execution
" of this will or codicil by the testator or
" testatrix, let it be inrolled in his Maje-
" sty's court of or in the court
" or office for inrolling deeds and wills in
" the county [or riding] of

" this

" this day of 178 .
" A. B. [or C. D and E. F.]"

Provided always, and be it further declared and enacted by the authority aforesaid, That in case all such attesting witnesses shall have died before the expiration of the time limited by this act for the inrolment of such will or codicil, then such *fiat*, warrant or direction to inrol may be granted by any such judge, master in Chancery, or justices of the peace, upon the oath or affidavit of any credible person, who shall have sworn to the handwriting of any such attesting witness as aforesaid; and in such case the form of every such *fiat*, warrant or direction shall be as followeth: Proviso in case of the deaths of attesting witnesses.

"Upon an oath having been made [or an "affidavit having been produced] before "me [or us] by A. B. that the name of "C. D. one of the attesting witnesses to "this will or codicil, is in the handwriting of the said C. D. who, as well as "the other attesting witnesses thereto, is "since dead, let this will [or codicil] be "inrolled in his Majesty's court of "or in the court or office for inrolling "deeds and wills in the county [or riding] "of this day of 178 Form of fiat in such case.

" A. B. [or A. B. and C. D]."

And it is hereby further declared and enacted by the authority aforesaid, That the subscription of the name or names of such judge, master in Chancery, or justices of the peace to any such *fiat*, warrant or direction for inrolment, written upon any such will or codicil, shall be a complete authority and warrant to the clerks, officers or commissioners of the respective courts or offices, to inrol such will or codicil, who, in case the said will or codicil, The fiat signed is the warrant to the clerk for inrolling.

upon

upon which ſuch *fiat*, warrant or direction ſhall appear ſubſcribed as aforeſaid, be properly ſtamped for inrolment, ſhall and are hereby required to inrol the ſame according to the directions and requiſitions of this act.

Proviſo in caſe of the loſs or ſuppreſſion of a will.

Provided always, and it is further declared and enacted by the authority aforeſaid, That in caſe of any mis-laying, concealment or ſuppreſſion of any ſuch will or codicil, the ſpace of ſix calendar months ſhall have elapſed from the death of the teſtator or teſtatrix, dying within the kingdom, or the ſpace of three years from ſuch death, in caſe of his or her dying without the kingdom as aforeſaid, it ſhall and may be lawful to and for any ſuch judge, maſter in Chancery, or juſtices of the peace, upon an oath or affidavit of the fact being made or produced before him or them to his or their ſatisfaction, to ſign any ſuch *fiat*, warrant or direction for inrolment, upon any ſuch will or codicil ſo having been miſlaid, concealed or ſuppreſſed as aforeſaid, although the time ſhall have elapſed, within which it ought to have been inrolled, in caſe it had not been ſo miſlaid, concealed or ſuppreſſed; and every ſuch inrolment ſhall be as good, valid and effectual, as if the will or codicil ſo miſlaid, concealed or ſuppreſſed had been inrolled within the time limited by this act, except as againſt purchaſers for a valuable conſideration, and all other incumbrancers without notice of ſuch will or codicil, where the purchaſe or incumbrance ſhall have been made after the death of the teſtator or teſtatrix, and before the actual inrolment of the will or codicil ſo miſlaid, concealed or ſuppreſſed.

And be it further declared and enacted by the authority aforeſaid, That every perſon procuring

curing ſuch acknowledgment of the execution of a deed or *fiat*, warrant or direction for the inrolment of a will or codicil, to be ſigned by ſuch judge, maſter in Chancery, or juſtices of the peace as aforeſaid, ſhall pay or cauſe to be paid the ſum of 5 s. to the perſon or perſons ſigning the ſame.

Fees for acknowledgments and fiats.

And be it further declared and enacted by the authority aforeſaid, That no ſuch deed, will nor codicil ſhall be inrolled as aforeſaid, which ſhall not have been properly ſtamped according to the intent and meaning of the 12th ſection of the 19th of his preſent Majeſty, c. 66. intituled, " *An act for granting to his Majeſty* " *ſeveral additional duties on ſtamped vellum,* " *parchment and paper, and for better ſecuring* " *the ſtamp duties upon indentures, leaſes, deeds* " *and other inſtruments*;" (that is to ſay) And it is hereby expreſsly declared to be the intention and meaning of the ſaid laſtmentioned act, as well as of this preſent act, that the number of ſtamps upon each deed, will or codicil, ſhall be proportioned to the number or quantity of words reſpectively contained therein, (that is to ſay); one proper ſtamp for inrolment for each deed, will or codicil, which ſhall contain a leſs number or quantity of words, than thirty common law ſheets, (each common law ſheet containing ſeventy-two words), and two ſuch ſtamps for each deed, will or codicil, which ſhall contain any number or quantity of words exceeding thirty common law ſheets, but leſs than forty-five ſuch common law ſheets; and ſo in proportion of one ſtamp for every fifteen common law ſheets of ſeventy-two words each, which ſuch deed, will or codicil ſhall contain over and above the number of fifteen common law ſheets, where the

Regulation of the number of ſtamps to be uſed.

the deed, will or codicil contains in the whole more, than thirty common law ſheets.

Confirmation of the practice of inrolling deeds in the courts of record.

Provided neverthelefs, and it is hereby expreſsly declared and enacted by the authority aforeſaid, That after ſuch acknowledgment of the execution of a deed, or ſuch *fiat*, warrant or direction for the inrolment of a will, ſhall have been ſigned by any ſuch judge, maſter in Chancery, or juſtices of the peace as aforeſaid, if the ſame ſhall be inrolled in any one of his Majeſty's courts of record at Weſtminſter, the ſame ſhall be inrolled therein in the manner and form, and for paying ſuch fees, as are now uſed and eſtabliſhed in each reſpective court, which uſages and eſtabliſhments are hereby allowed, ratified and confirmed.

Mode of inrolling in the county courts.

And be it further declared and enacted by the authority aforeſaid, That every ſuch deed, will or codicil, ſo to be inrolled in any court or office of inrolment in the county, riding or diviſion, in which the lands, tenements or hereditaments compriſed in or affected by ſuch deed, will or codicil, are ſituate, lying and being, ſhall be firſt fairly and faithfully written or ingroſſed upon proper rolls of parchment of one uniform ſize and dimenſion; which parchment ſhall be provided by the clerks, officers or commiſſioners of the different courts or offices, and ſhall be by them delivered *gratis* to all perſons applying for the ſame, for the purpoſe of inrolling any deed, will or codicil thereupon in their reſpective court or offices; and when any ſuch deed will or codicil ſhall have been ſo written or ingroſſed upon the rolls, and ſhall have been examined with, and found to be a true and faithful copy of the original deed, will or codicil,

dicil, by the perſon bringing the ſame to be inrolled, and one of the clerks, officers or commiſſioners of ſuch court or office, or his or their deputy or deputies, in caſe there ſhall be the proper number of ſtamps by the aforeſaid act paſſed in the 19th year of his ſaid preſent Majeſty, and hereby required upon the deed, will or codicil ſo to be inrolled, then ſuch deed, will or codicil, ſhall be inrolled or entered upon or amongſt the rolls of ſuch court or office, there to remain a record of ſuch court or office; and the clerk, officer or commiſſioner of the reſpective court or office, or his deputy or deputies, ſhall thereupon indorſe upon every ſuch deed, will or codicil, a certificate of the time of inrolling the ſame, and ſign ſuch indorſed certificate.

£. 50 penalties upon officers inrolling without a proper number of ſtamps.

Provided always, and be it further declared and enacted by the authority aforeſaid, That in caſe any ſuch clerk, officer or commiſſioner, or his or their deputy or deputies, ſhall inrol or ſuffer to be inrolled, any deed, will or codicil, which ſhall not have been ſtamped, according to the directions and requiſitions of the ſaid act of the nineteenth year of the reign of his ſaid preſent Majeſty, and of this act, every ſuch defaulter or defaulters ſhall forfeit the ſum of £. 50 of lawful money of Great Britain, with treble coſts of ſuit for every fifteen common law ſheets, which ſhall be contained in any ſuch deed, will or codicil, over and above the quantity or number of words, thereby and hereby allowed of or limited to each ſtamp, to any perſon or perſons who ſhall within five years after the inrolment of any ſuch deed, will or codicil, without the requiſite number of ſtamps, inform or ſue for the ſame, in any court of record within the king-

To be recovered upon information within five years.

dom of England or dominion of Wales, by action of debt, bill, plaint or information, wherein no essoign, protection, nor wager of law shall be allowed.

Where deeds and wills affecting lands lying in divers counties may be inrolled.

And be it further declared and enacted by the authority aforesaid, That wherever any one deed, will or codicil shall concern, relate to or affect lands, tenements or hereditaments, situate, lying and being in divers counties, ridings or divisions, it shall be at the option of the person or persons inrolling the same, to inrol such deed, will or codicil, in any of the four courts of record at Westminster, or in any court or office of a county, riding or division, in which any of the said lands, tenements or hereditaments, comprised in or affected by such deed, will or codicil, shall be situate, lying and being.

Where lands lying in divers counties are affected by one deed or will, abstracts to be entered in each respective county court.

And be it further declared and enacted by the authority aforesaid, That wherever any deed, will or codicil, shall have been inrolled in any of his Majesty's four courts of record at Westminster, or in any county court or office of inrolment, where the lands, tenements or hereditaments comprised in or affected by such deed, will or codicil, shall be in divers counties, ridings or divisions, then an abstract of so much of such deed, will or codicil, as relates to, concerns or affects the lands, tenements or hereditaments, situate, lying and being in any particular county, riding or division, in which such deed, will or codicil shall not be inrolled, shall within the space of three calendar months, to be computed from the time, at which such deed, will or codicil ought to be inrolled, be entered or inrolled in the county court or office, in which such lands, tenements or hereditaments, comprised comprifed in or affected by fuch deed, will or codicil, are fituate, lying and being refpectively: and every fuch abftract fo to be entered or inrolled, fhall be written or ingroffed upon vellum or parchment (to be provided and delivered by the clerks, officers or commiffioners, in manner aforefaid) in a fair, legible hand; and fhall contain the date of the deed, will or codicil, the names of the parties to fuch deed, or the name and defcription of the teftator or teftatrix of any fuch will or codicil, and a fufficient defcription of the parcels to afcertain the lands, tenements or hereditaments, fituate, lying and being within the refpective county, riding or divifion, in the court or office of which, fuch abftract fhall be entered, and the ufes, limitations, trufts, charges, powers, conditions, provifoes and agreements, by which fuch lands, tenements and hereditaments are affected, and the execution of the different parties, who fhall have executed the fame, and the time at which, and the court or office, in which fuch deed, will or codicil fhall have been inrolled: And before any fuch abftract fhall be entered as aforefaid, the original deed fo inrolled, or the original will or codicil, or a probate thereof fhall be produced to the commiffioners, officers or clerks, or their fufficient deputy or deputies, who after having examined fuch abftract with the original deed, will or codicil, or probate, and found the fame to be a faithful and true abftract thereof refpectively, fhall indorfe upon fuch deed, will, codicil or probate, a certificate under his or their hand or hands, that a true abftract of fo much thereof hath been entered in their refpective court or office, as relateth

What each abftract fhall contain.

Certificates of the abftracts to be indorfed upon the deed, will or codicil, or probate.

to or concerneth any lands, tenements or hereditaments, over which their refpective court or office extendeth.

Fees for entering abftracts.

And be it further declared and enacted by the authority aforefaid, That the commiffioners, officers or clerks, fhall be allowed for the entry of every fuch abftract, as is by this act directed and required to be entered, the fum of twopence and no more, for every common law fheet of feventy-two words each fheet, and fo in proportion for a greater or lefs quantity or number of words, which fuch abftract fhall contain.

The certificate indorfed upon inrolled deeds to be evidence of the inrolment.

And be it further declared and enacted by the authority aforefaid, That all deeds, wills and codicils, fo inrolled either in any of the faid courts of record at Weftminfter, or in any of the faid courts or offices for inrolling the fame in the different counties, ridings or divifions as aforefaid, which fhall appear to be fo inrolled by certificate of fuch inrolment, indorfed upon any fuch deed, will or codicil, and figned by the proper clerk, officer or commiffioner refpectively, fhall be taken and allowed as evidence of fuch inrolment, in all courts of record and elfewhere.

Office copies of inrolments to be evidence, where the original not forthcoming.

And it is further declared and enacted by the authority aforefaid, That in all cafes, in which any perfon or perfons claiming under any deed, will or codicil inrolled, fhall not have the poffeffion, cuftody, nor power of the original deed, nor of the will, codicil, or probate thereof, then where in any declaration, avowry, bar, replication or other pleading whatfoever, any fuch deed, will or codicil inrolled, fhall be pleaded with a *profert in curiâ*, or offer to produce the fame, the perfon or perfons fo pleading, fhall and may produce and

and ſhew forth, and be ſuffered and allowed to produce and ſhew forth, by the authority of this act, to anſwer ſuch *profert*, as well againſt his Majeſty, his heirs and ſucceſſors, as againſt any other perſon or perſons whomſoever, a copy of the inrolment of ſuch deed, will or codicil; and ſuch copy examined with the inrolment, and ſigned by the proper clerk, officer or commiſſioner, and proved upon oath to be a true copy ſo examined and ſigned, ſhall be of the ſame force and effect, to all intents and conſtructions of law and equity, as the original deed, will or codicil inrolled, would or ſhould be of, if the ſame were in any ſuch caſe produced and ſhewn forth in any court of record or elſewhere.

Offices to be eſtabliſhed.

And be it further declared and enacted by the authority aforeſaid, That there ſhall be erected and eſtabliſhed public offices for inrolling and preſerving the rolls and abſtracts of all deeds, wills and codicils within the time, in the manner, and at the places hereinafter limited, directed and appointed; (that is to ſay) before the day of 1789, there ſhall be conſtructed a ſtrong and dry building or repoſitory, ſo detached from any other buildings, as to render the ſame ſecure from fire or other accidents, in which ſuch rolls may be ſafely depoſited, and ſo near unto the court or office for inrolling deeds, wills and codicils, that the ſame may be daily depoſited therein at ſuch hours, at which they ſhall not be kept open for public inſpection, examination or uſe, at each of the following places, in which all deeds, wills and codicils, or abſtracts thereof relating to, touching or affecting lands, tenements and hereditaments, ſituate, lying and being within the counties, divifions or ridings, hereinafter mentioned, fhall be inrolled or entered refpectively, (that is to fay):

At Bedford for the county of Bedford.

At Reading for the county of Berks.

At Aylefbury for the county of Bucks.

At Cambridge for the county of Cambridge.

At Chefter for the county of Chefter, with the city and county of the city of Chefter.

At Launcefton for the county of Cornwall.

At Carlifle for the county of Cumberland.

At Derby for the county of Derby.

At Exeter for the county of Devon, with the city and county of the city of Exeter.

At Dorchefter for the county of Dorfet, with the city and county of the city of Pool.

At Durham for the county palatine of Durham.

At Chelmsford for the county of Effex.

At Gloucefter for the county of Gloucefter, with the city and county of the city of Gloucefter, and the city and county of the city of Briftol.

At Hereford for the county of Hereford.

At Hertford for the county of Hertford.

At Huntingdon for the county of Huntingdon.

At Canterbury for the county of Kent, and the county of the city of Canterbury.

At Prefton for the county palatine of Lancafter.

At Leicefter for the county of Leicefter.

At Lincoln for the county of Lincoln.

At London for the county of Middlefex.

At Monmouth for the county of Monmouth.

At Norwich for the county of Norfolk, with the city and county of the city of Norwich.

At

At Northampton for the county of Northampton.

At Newcaſtle upon Tyne for the county of Northumberland, with the town and county of the town of Newcaſtle upon Tyne and the town of Berwick upon Tweed.

At Oxford for the county of Oxford.

At Oakham for the county of Rutland.

At Shrewſbury for the county of Salop.

At Taunton for the county of Somerſet.

At Wincheſter for the county of Southampton, with the town and county of the town of Southampton.

At Stafford for the county of Stafford, with the county and city of Litchfield.

At Ipſwich for the county of Suffolk.

At Guilford for the county of Surry.

At Chicheſter for the county of Suſſex.

At Warwick for the county of Warwick, with the city and county of the city of Coventry.

At Kendal for the county of Weſtmoreland.

At Worceſter for the county of Worceſter, with the city and county of Worceſter.

At Saliſbury for the county of Wilts.

At Wakefield for the weſt-riding of the county of York.

At Northarlerton for the north-riding of the county of York.

At Beverley for the eaſt-riding of the county of York, with the town and county of the town of Kingſton upon Hull.

At Beaumaris for the county of Angleſea.

At Brecon for the county of Brecknock.

At Cardigan for the county of Cardigan.

At Carmarthen for the county of Carmarthen, and county borough of Carmarthen.

At Caernarvon for the county of Caernarvon.

At Denbigh for the county of Denbigh.

At

At Flint for the county of Flint.
At Cardiff for the county of Glamorgan.
At Bala for the county of Merioneth.
At Montgomery for the county of Montgomery.
At Pembroke for the county of Pembroke, and town and county of Haverford West.
At Radnor for the county of Radnor.

County courts or offices how to be built and repaired.

All which ſaid buildings, repoſitories, courts or offices, ſhall be purchaſed, built, repaired and eſtabliſhed at the public charge of each county, diviſion or diſtrict reſpectively, to be raiſed by the juſtices of the peace thereof, at the general quarter ſeſſions of the peace, in ſuch manner, as they are empowered to raiſe money for the repairs of public or county bridges, and in ſuch places, as to the majority of the ſaid juſtices of the peace, at their general quarter ſeſſions, ſhall ſeem moſt proper and convenient.

The officers or clerks how to be elected.

And be it further declared and enacted by the authority aforeſaid, That the ſaid officers, commiſſioners, or clerks for managing and conducting the buſineſs of ſuch offices or courts, ſhall be appointed in manner following (that is to ſay): At the firſt general quarter ſeſſions of the peace, which ſhall be holden for the reſpective county, riding or diviſion, in which a court or office is to be erected or eſtabliſhed, after the day of 1789, every perſon repreſenting in parliament the county, or any city or borough within the diſtrict, over which the reſpective inrolment-court or office ſhall extend, ſhall either attend in perſon, or by ſome fit perſon authoriſed and empowered under a proper power of attorney, ſealed, ſigned and delivered by ſuch

ſuch abſentee, in the preſence of two credible perſons, and ſhall there deliver in to the ſaid court of quarter ſeſſion, a paper in the hand-writing of ſuch abſent elector, containing the name, quality and deſcription of the perſon, whom he chuſes and elects for the clerk, officer or commiſſioner of the inrolment-court or office of that reſpective diſtrict; and in caſe of ſuch elector appearing by deputy, proxy or attorney, the oath of ſuch deputy, proxy or attorney ſhall be taken in open court, that the paper delivered into court was ſigned and ſealed by the abſent elector in his preſence: And the perſon, who ſhall have a majority of ſuch votes, ſhall be declared by the ſaid court to be duly elected the commiſſioner, officer or clerk of the ſaid inrolment-court or office; and ſhall from thenceforth be duly appointed, and ſhall continue in ſuch commiſſion, charge or office, for ſo long a time, as he ſhall well and faithfully demean himſelf therein; and in caſe any two or more perſons ſhall have an equal number of votes, then the majority ſhall be decided by the votes of the major part of the juſtices of the peace, (not being any of them members of parliament) who ſhall be then upon the bench; and in caſe they ſhall be divided into equal numbers, then the ſenior juſtice ſhall have the caſting vote.

The regiſters of the three ridings of the county of York to remain till death or vacation.

Provided nevertheleſs, and it is hereby further declared and enacted by the authority aforeſaid, That no ſuch election as aforeſaid ſhall be had or made for any officer, clerk or commiſſioner, for any of the inrolment-offices within the three ridings of the county of York, until the death, reſignation, ſurrender or vacation of the preſent regiſters, or any of

them,

them, but they ſhall continue from thenceforth ſo long as they ſhall well demean themſelves in their ſaid reſpective offices, commiſſions or charges, but ſhall from the day of 1789 regulate, perform and execute the buſineſs of their reſpective courts or offices, according to the tenor, requiſitions and intentions of this act; and all future officers, clerks or commiſſioners for the ſaid ridings ſhall be elected and choſen in the manner hereby directed and required.

Who to be the clerks for the office for Middleſex.

Provided alſo, and it is further declared and enacted by the authority aforeſaid, That from and after the day of 1789, the regiſter-office for the county of Middleſex ſhall be converted into the court or office for inrolling all deeds, wills and codicils affecting lands, tenements and hereditaments, lying within the ſaid county, and the ſworn clerk to execute the office of inrolment in the high court of Chancery, who is appointed to inrol for the county of Middleſex, the chief clerk to inrol pleas in the King's Bench, the clerk of the warrants in the court of Common-Pleas, and the King's remembrancer or his deputy in the court of Exchequer, ſhall be the clerks, officers or commiſſioners of the ſaid inrolment-court or office for the county of Middleſex; and they ſhall and may from time to time nominate and appoint one or more able and ſufficient perſon or perſons, for whom they ſhall be accountable and reſponſible, to be their deputy or deputies; and they ſhall continue to be nominated and appointed in the manner, in which they have heretofore uſually been nominated and appointed; and they ſhall regulate, perform and execute the buſineſs of ſuch inrolment-court or or office, for the ſaid county of Middleſex, according to the tenor, requiſitions and intentions of this act.

Penalty on officers neglecting duty.

And be it further declared and enacted by the authority aforeſaid, That if any ſuch officers, commiſſioners or clerks, either by themſelves or by their deputies, ſhall neglect to perform his or their duty in the execution of their ſaid offices, charges or commiſſions, according to the regulations and forms by this act directed and required, or commit or exerciſe, or ſuffer or procure to be committed or exerciſed, any undue or fraudulent practice in the execution of their ſaid offices, charges or commiſſions, and be thereof lawfully convicted, then ſuch clerk, officer or commiſſioner ſhall forfeit his ſaid office, charge or commiſſion, and pay treble damages with full coſts of ſuit, to every ſuch perſon or perſons, as ſhall be injured thereby, to be recovered by action of debt, bill, plaint or information, in any of his Majeſty's courts of record at Weſtminſter, wherein no eſſoign, protection, privilege, nor wager of law ſhall be allowed, nor any more than one imparlance.

Oath to be taken by the officers or clerks.

And it is further declared and enacted by the authority aforeſaid, That all and every ſuch perſon and perſons ſo to be elected, nominated or appointed as aforeſaid, before they or he ſhall enter upon the execution of the ſaid office, employment or charge as aforeſaid, ſhall be ſworn before one or more of the juſtices of any of his Majeſty's courts of record at Weſtminſter, or before three or more of the juſtices of the peace for the county, riding, diviſion or diſtrict, for which they or he ſhall be ſo elected, nominated or appointed commiſſioners, officers or clerks as aforeſaid, who are hereby authorifed, empowered and required to adminifter fuch oath in the following words, (that is to fay).

"I *A. B.* having been elected, nominated "or appointed a commiffioner, officer "or clerk for executing and managing "the court or office of inrolling deeds, "wills and codicils, within the county "[or riding] of do hereby "folemnly fwear, that I will duly, juft-"ly and faithfully perform and execute "the faid office, charge or commiffion, "according to the tenor, directions and "requifitions of an act of parliament "made in the 29th year of his Majefty "King George the Third, intituled, "" *An act for requiring the inrolment of* "*all deeds, wills and codicils relating to,* "*touching or affecting any freehold and* "*leafehold lands, tenements or heredita-*"*ments, within the kingdom of England,* "*dominion of Wales, and for other pur-*"*pofes therein mentioned,*" according to "the beft of my judgment and the dic-"tates of my confcience.

" So help me GOD."

And to find two fureties to enter into recognizances of £.6000 each.

And be it further declared and enacted by the authority aforefaid, That every fuch commiffioner, officer or clerk fo to be elected, nominated or appointed as aforefaid, before his admiffion to fuch office, employment or charge, fhall find two fufficient fureties, who fhall enter into feparate recognizances, before the lord high chancellor of England, or the chief juftice of his Majefty's court of King's Bench or of the Common Pleas, or of the chief baron of his Majefty's court of Exchequer at Weftminfter, wherein they fhall become

come ſeverally and reſpectively bounden to his Majeſty, his heirs and ſucceſſors, in the ſum of £. 6000 each, for the punctual and faithful execution of the ſaid office, employment or charge, by the perſon ſo to be elected, nominated or appointed, for whom they ſhall have entered into ſuch ſecurity as aforeſaid.

Recognizances to become void in three years after death or vacation.

Provided nevertheleſs, and be it further declared and enacted by the authority aforeſaid, That when any ſuch commiſſioner, officer or clerk ſhall die, or ſurrender or vacate his office, charge or commiſſion, and if within the ſpace of three years from and after ſuch death, ſurrender or vacation, no miſbehaviour appear to have been committed by ſuch officer, clerk or commiſſioner, in the execution of his ſaid office, charge or commiſſion, then and in ſuch caſe, at the end of the ſaid three years after ſuch death, ſurrender or vacation, the ſaid recognizance ſo entered into ſhall become void and of none effect, to all intents and purpoſes whatſoever.

Fees for inrolling.

And be it further declared and enacted by the authority aforeſaid, That from and after the day of in the year of our Lord 1789, it ſhall and may be lawful to and for ſuch commiſſioners, officers or clerks for the time being, to aſk and demand from every perſon inrolling any ſuch deed, will or codicil as aforeſaid, the ſum of threepence for every common law ſheet or folio, and ſo in proportion for a greater or leſs number contained in the deed, will or codicil ſo to be inrolled; and alſo one ſhilling for every certificate, which they ſhall indorſe upon any ſuch deed, will or codicil, as hereinbefore they were directed to do.

And

Office to be open for fearches. And be it further declared and enacted by the authority aforefaid, That the faid feveral entries and inrolments fhall be kept in fuch courts or offices open for the infpection of all perfons, upon all days (except Sundays and holydays) throughout the year, from the hour of ten o'clock in the forenoon till three o'clock in the afternoon of the fame day; and the faid commiffioners, officers or clerks for the time being, and their deputies, are hereby authorifed and empowered to demand the fum of one fhilling from every perfon, for each fearch, which he or fhe fhall chufe to make; and alfo to demand the fum of five fhillings for every fifteen common law fheets, which they fhall be required to make an extract or copy of, and fo in proportion for a greater or lefs number of words.

Fees for fearches,

and for copies.

Office copies to be ftamped as in Chancery. Provided neverthelefs, and it is hereby further declared and enacted by the authority aforefaid, That no fuch office-copy of the whole or any part of any fuch deed, will or codicil fhall be made, but upon fuch ftamps, as are directed and required to be put upon all office copies of deeds, wills or proceedings made in any of the offices connected with or dependant upon the high court of Chancery.

Books to be kept regularly and orderly. And be it further declared and enacted by the authority aforefaid, That in every fuch court or office for inrolling deeds, wills and codicils as aforefaid, the clerk, officer or commiffioner of fuch refpective court or office fhall, as he is hereby bounden to the faithful difcharge of his office, charge or commiffion, to keep and preferve proper books, in which entries fhall be made of all deeds, wills and codicils, and of all abftracts, that have been inrolled or entered in that particular court or

 office;

office: And every ſuch entry ſhall ſet forth the date of the deed, will or codicil, or abſtract, and the name and names of the granting or covenanting party or parties to the deed, or of the teſtator or teſtatrix, and the time, at which the ſame was inrolled or entered.

The fees, how to be applied.

And be it further declared and enacted by the authority aforeſaid, That all ſuch payments hereby directed to be made into the ſaid courts or offices, ſhall be paid unto and received by the commiſſioners, officers or clerks for the time being, for their care, management and cuſtody of ſuch inrolments and entries, and for attending by themſelves or deputies, at ſuch hours during which the ſaid courts or offices are hereby directed to be kept open as aforeſaid, and for computing and examining all ſuch deeds, wills, codicils and abſtracts, and for making extracts and copies thereof, and alſo for making and keeping ſuch books of entries and references, and alſo for collecting and making out ſuch entries of all deeds, wills, codicils and abſtracts, and tranſmitting the ſame every half-year to the clerk, officer or commiſſioner of the reference office in London, as is hereinafter mentioned, and alſo for paying and diſcharging all the coſts, charges and expences of all the parchment and paper uſed in their reſpective courts or offices, and alſo for paying and diſcharging whatever yearly or other payments, rents, taxes, impoſitions or aſſeſſments ſhall from time to time become due and payable, for and in reſpect of the houſes, buildings and premiſſes, in which ſuch courts or offices, and repoſitories ſhall be, and alſo whatever monies ſhall from time to time be required to keep the ſame in con-

 ſtant,

ſtant, good and ſubſtantial repairs, and alſo for defraying all the expences, coſts and charges, which ſhall be incurred by the poſtage and carriage of letters, packets and parcels, and generally by all other matters relative to the buſineſs of the ſaid courts or offices.

A reference office to be eſtabliſhed.

And in order, that perſons having occaſion to ſearch the different courts or offices for the inrolment of ſuch deeds, wills and codicils, may do the ſame with the greater eaſe, certainty and ſatisfaction; be it further declared and enacted by the authority aforeſaid, That from and after the day of in the year 1789, there ſhall be erected or purchaſed and eſtabliſhed a *reference office* in or near in the ſaid county of Middleſex, at the joint expences and by equal contribution of each county, riding and diviſion throughout England and Wales, in which any ſuch court or office is or ſhall be eſtabliſhed as aforeſaid.

King to appoint clerks of the reference office.

And it is further declared and enacted by the authority aforeſaid, That it ſhall and may be lawful to and for the King's Majeſty, his heirs and ſucceſſors to nominate and appoint by commiſſion, to be iſſued under the great ſeal of Great Britain, ſuch two perſons, as his Majeſty ſhall think fit to be the officers, clerks or commiſſioners, for managing, conducting and executing the buſineſs of ſuch reference office by themſelves, or their ſufficient deputy or deputies, and who ſhall continue in ſuch office, charge or commiſſion ſo long, as they ſhall well and faithfully demean themſelves therein; and they ſhall before their admiſſion to ſuch office, charge or commiſſion, find two ſufficient ſureties, who ſhall enter into ſeparate recognizances, before the lord high Chancellor

The clerks to find two ſureties, to enter into recognizances of 3,000 l. each.

cellor of England, or the lord chief Justice of his Majesty's court of King's Bench, or of the Common Pleas at Westminster, or the lord chief Baron of his Majesty's court of Exchequer, wherein they shall become respectively bounden to his Majesty, his heirs and successors, in the sum of £. 3000 each, for the punctual and faithful execution of the said office, charge or commission, by the persons so to be nominated, appointed and commissioned as aforesaid: And such officers, clerk or commissioners, shall also before their admission to the said office, charge or commission, before the lord high Chancellor of England, or the chief Justice of his Majesty's court of King's Bench, or of the Common Pleas, at Westminster, or of the chief Baron of his Majesty's court of Exchequer, take and subscribe an oath in the form following; that is to say—

And take the oath of office.

"I A. B. having been appointed by his Majesty's commission, under the great seal of Great Britain, an officer, clerk or commissioner of the reference office, do hereby solemnly swear, that I will duly, justly and faithfully execute the said office, charge or commission, according to the tenor, condition, and requisitions of the act of the 29th year of the reign of his Majesty King George III. intituled, "*An act for requiring the inrolment of all deeds, wills and codicils, relating to, touching or affecting any freehold or leasehold lands, tenements or hereditaments within the kingdom of England and dominion of Wales, and for other purposes therein mentioned.*" So help me God."

And it is further declared and enacted by the authority aforesaid, That separate and distinct

The books, how to be kept.

diſtinct books for each county, riding or diviſion, in which a court or office is or ſhall be erected or eſtabliſhed, ſhall be kept and preſerved in the reference office, in which entries ſhall be made of all deeds, wills and codicils, and of all abſtracts, that have been inrolled or entered in any of the courts of record, or county courts or offices reſpectively as aforeſaid; and every ſuch entry ſhall ſet forth the date of the deed, will or codicil or abſtract, and the name or names of the grantor or grantors, grantee or grantees, or of the teſtator or teſtatrix, and the county or counties, in which the lands, tenements or hereditaments affected by ſuch deed, will or codicil lie, and the court in which, and the time, at which the ſame was inrolled or entered.

One ſhilling to be paid for each deed towards the reference office.

And it is further declared and enacted, by the authority aforeſaid, That every perſon inrolling or cauſing to be inrolled or entered any deed, will or codicil or abſtract as aforeſaid, in any of the ſaid courts of record, or in any of the ſaid county courts or offices, is hereby required to pay one ſhilling over and above all other payments hereby directed and required to be made as aforeſaid, for every ſuch deed, will or codicil or abſtract, ſo inrolled or entered as aforeſaid, unto the clerk, officer or commiſſioner of the court, in which ſuch deed, will or codicil or abſtract, is reſpectively inrolled or entered.

Entries to be tranſmitted once in every month to the reference office.

And it is further enacted and declared by the authority aforeſaid, That the officers, commiſſioners or clerks of the different county courts, are hereby directed and required, in conſideration of the aforeſaid emoluments and perquiſites hereby allowed unto them, to tranſmit once in every month, ſuch entries of the different deeds, wills, codicils and abſtracts,

ſtracts, as have been inrolled and entered in their reſpective court or office, to the officers clerks or commiſſioners of the ſaid reference office, who are alſo hereby required to enter the ſame forthwith in the ſeveral and reſpective books, in the manner and form aforeſaid; and to pay or tranſmit, or cauſe to be paid or tranſmitted, at the ſame time, the ſum of one ſhilling unto the clerks, commiſſioners or officers of the ſaid reference office, which they ſhall have received in manner aforeſaid: And the ſaid officers, clerks or commiſſioners of the ſaid reference office, ſhall once in every month, make or cauſe to be made, an extract or entry of every deed, will or codicil, inrolled in any of the ſaid courts of record at Weſtminſter; and they ſhall receive from the clerks, officers or commiſſioners of the reſpective courts, in which ſuch deed, will or codicil ſhall be inrolled, the ſum of one ſhilling for each deed, will, codicil or abſtract, which ſhall have been received by them, at the time of their original inrolment or entry reſpectively; all which extracts or entries ſhall be fairly written and regularly entered in the books for the different counties for that purpoſe kept in the ſaid reference office.

The clerks of the reference office to extract monthly all deeds and wills inrolled in the courts of record.

The entries to be made in the books of the reference office.

And it is further declared and enacted by the authority aforeſaid, That from and after the ſaid day of in the year 1789, whenever a judgment, ſtatute or recognizance, (other than and except ſuch, as ſhall be entered in the name and upon the proper account of his Majeſty, his heirs or ſucceſſors) ſhall be obtained or entered into, of or concerning, or whereby any freehold or leaſehold lands, tenements or hereditaments, within the

Notice to be given in writing at the reference office of judgments, ſtatutes and recognizances.

 kingdom

kingdom of England, or dominion of Wales, can, ſhall or may be in any manner affected, in law or equity, the plaintiff or plaintiffs, conuſee or conuſees, ſhall within the ſpace of three days after the entering up of any ſuch judgment or acknowledgment of any ſuch ſtatute or recognizance, is and are hereby required to give notice thereof in writing to the clerks, officers or commiſſioners of the ſaid reference office; and every ſuch notice, which ſhall be ſigned by the clerk or clerks of the court, in which ſuch judgment, ſtatute or recognizance ſhall be recorded reſpectively, ſhall contain the name or names of the plaintiff or plaintiffs, and defendant or defendants, conuſor or conuſors, and conuſee or conuſees, in ſuch judgment, ſtatute or recognizance reſpectively; the day, on which ſuch judgment ſhall have been entered up, or ſuch ſtatute or recognizance ſhall have been acknowledged, and the amount of the ſum or ſums of money, for which ſuch judgment ſhall have been obtained, or ſuch ſtatute or recognizance ſhall have been acknowledged reſpectively; and the county, riding or diviſion, in which any lands, tenements or hereditaments are ſituate, lying and being, which are affected thereby in law or equity: And the clerks, officers or commiſſioners of the ſaid office, ſhall and are hereby required to make entries thereof, in the reſpective books of the ſaid reference office; and ſhall and are alſo hereby required within the ſpace of three days, to be computed from the time of their receiving ſuch notice or notices, to tranſmit a copy or copies of the entry of every ſuch judgment, ſtatute or recognizance, to the clerk, officer or commiſſioner of the court or office, within the

Entries thereof to be made.

the diſtrict of which, any of the lands, tenements or hereditaments, ſo affected by the judgment, ſtatute or recognizance as aforeſaid, are ſituate, lying and being, in order that a proper entry may be made of ſuch judgment, ſtatute or recognizance, in the books of each court or office, by the reſpective clerk, officer or commiſſioner thereof, who in conſideration of the allowances hereby made to him and them, is and are hereby required to enter ſuch copies ſo tranſmitted to them in their reſpective books.

Provided always, and it is further declared and enacted by the authority aforeſaid, That no ſuch judgment, ſtatute nor recognizance, ſhall in any manner affect any lands, tenements or hereditaments, of or concerning which, ſuch notice ſhall not have been given to or left with the clerks, officers or commiſſioners of the ſaid reference office as aforeſaid.

No land to be affected by a judgment, &c. unleſs notice left at the reference office.

And it is further declared and enacted by the authority aforeſaid, That the clerks, officers or commiſſioners of the ſaid reference office, are hereby authorized and empowered to demand of and from ſuch plaintiff or plaintiffs, conuſee or conuſees, the ſum of one ſhilling for each county, riding or diviſion, to the court or office of which, they are hereby required to ſend or tranſmit ſuch notice of any judgment, ſtatute or recognizance as aforeſaid.

Fee of one ſhilling for the clerks tranſmitting the notice to each county court.

And it is further declared and enacted by the authority aforeſaid, That from and after the day of in the year of our Lord 1789, in caſe the whole or any part of the money ſecured under or by virtue of any deed, will, codicil, judgment, ſtatute or recog-

Satisfactions how to be entered and certified.

 nizance,

nizance, which ſhall have been ſo inrolled or entered as aforeſaid, ſhall be paid off, ſatisfied or diſcharged, if at any time or times afterwards a certificate ſhall be brought to the clerk, officer or commiſſioner of the court or office, in which ſuch inrolment or entry ſhall have been made, ſigned by the perſon or perſons entitled to receive ſuch monies, and atteſted by two credible witneſſes ſpecifying the amount of the monies paid off, ſatisfied and diſcharged, (which witneſſes ſhall upon their oath before any one of the Judges of his Majeſty's court of King's Bench or Common Pleas, or any one of the Barons of the court of Exchequer, or before any one of the maſters of the court of Chancery, or before any two or more juſtices of the peace, or before the clerk, officer or commiſſioner of the court or office, in which ſuch deed, will, codicil, judgment, ſtatute or recognizance ſhall have been inrolled or entered reſpectively, who are hereby reſpectively impowered to adminiſter ſuch oath, prove ſuch monies to have been paid off, ſatisfied or diſcharged accordingly, and that they ſaw ſuch certificate ſigned by the perſon or perſons intitled to receive the ſame) and then in every ſuch caſe, the clerk, officer or commiſſioner, or his or their deputy or deputies, ſhall make an entry in the margin, or at the foot of every ſuch roll of a deed, will or codicil, and in the margin of every book oppoſite to the entry of every judgment, ſtatute or recognizance, under or by virtue of which, the monies ſo paid off, ſatisfied or diſcharged, ſhall have been ſecured or made payable, that the ſame have been paid off, ſatisfied and diſcharged according to ſuch certificate, to which the ſame roll or entry ſhall refer; and

ſhall

ſhall after file ſuch certificate to remain upon record in the ſaid court or office: and all ſuch clerks, officers or commiſſioners are hereby authorized and impowered to demand the ſum of one ſhilling from every perſon or perſons bringing ſuch certificate, to be entered and filed as aforeſaid.

The books to be open for ſearches.

And it is further declared and enacted by the authority aforeſaid, That the ſaid ſeveral books of entries or extracts ſhall be kept in the ſaid reference office open for the inſpection of all perſons, upon all days (except Sundays and holydays) throughout the year, from the hour of ten of the clock in the forenoon, 'till three of the clock in the afternoon of the ſame day: And the officers, clerks or commiſſioners for the time being, of the ſaid reference office, and their deputies, are hereby authorized and impowered to demand the ſum of one ſhilling from every perſon, for each ſearch, which he or they ſhall make; and alſo to demand the like ſum of one ſhilling, for every entry or extract, which they ſhall be required to make a copy of.

Fees for ſearches and copies.

Application of fees.

And it is further declared and enacted, by the authority aforeſaid, That as well the monies paid or remitted to the clerks, officers or commiſſioners of the ſaid reference office, at the time of their taking or receiving ſuch entries or extracts as aforeſaid, as the monies received for all ſearches and copies as aforeſaid, ſhall be allowed unto the ſaid clerks, officers or commiſſioners, for attending and collecting ſuch entries or extracts from the ſaid courts of record in manner aforeſaid; and for purchaſing, digeſting and keeping the aforeſaid books, and making ſuch entries and extracts therein, and for attending the ſaid office

office at the hours before mentioned, and for defraying the expences and charges of keeping one or more deputy or deputies, and alſo for paying and diſcharging whatever yearly or other payments, rents, taxes or aſſeſſments, ſhall from time to time become due and payable, for and in reſpect of the houſe, buildings, and premiſſes, in which the ſaid reference office ſhall be, and alſo whatever monies ſhall from time to time be required to keep the ſame in conſtant, good and ſubſtantial repair, and alſo for defraying all the expences, coſts and charges, which ſhall be incurred by the poſtage or carriage of letters, packets and parcels, and generally by all other matters neceſſarily relating to, touching or concerning the ſaid reference office.

Members of parliament not eligible.

And be it further declared and enacted by the authority aforeſaid, That no member of parliament for the time being, of any county, city or borough, ſhall be capable of being choſen clerk, officer or commiſſioner of any ſuch court or office of a county, riding or diviſion, or of the reference office, or of executing by himſelf or any other perſon, ſuch office, or have, take or receive any fee or other profit whatever, for or in reſpect thereof; nor ſhall any ſuch clerk, officer or commiſſioner, or his or their deputy or deputies for the time being, be capable of being choſen to ſerve in parliament.

Recital.

And whereas it ſometimes happeneth, that wills and codicils are deſtroyed, miſlaid, loſt or ſuppreſſed, by accident, neglect or deſign, whereby the rights of your Majeſty's liege ſubjects, who might have claimed under ſuch wills and codicils, are defeated; and whereas

whereas it may be ſatisfactory for many perſons having made wills or codicils to wills, or other teſtamentary diſpoſitions or inſtructions, that the ſame may be depoſited during their lives, in ſome ſecure repoſitory, and that no perſon, but the teſtator or teſtatrix can have acceſs during his or her life to ſuch wills or codicils, and no other but the proper perſon or perſons can have acceſs to or acquire the poſſeſſion thereof after their deaths; be it therefore declared and enacted, by the authority aforeſaid, That from and after the day of in the year of our Lord 1789, the ſaid clerks, officers or commiſſioners of the ſaid reference office ſhall prepare and diſtribute into alphabetical and chronological order, an apartment in the ſaid reference office, in which all wills or codicils, or teſtamentary diſpoſitions or inſtructions which ſhall be brought to the ſaid office, ſhall be depoſited, and ſafely and orderly kept, until the ſame ſhall be required to be delivered out in manner hereinafter mentioned.

The clerks to provide an apartment in the reference office, for depoſiting wills.

And be it further declared and enacted, by the authority aforeſaid, That if any perſon chuſing to leave or depoſit his or her will or codicil, or teſtamentary diſpoſition or inſtructions in the ſaid office, ſhall bring the ſame to the ſaid clerks, officers or commiſſioners, and pay the ſum of 2s. 6d. to ſuch clerks, officers or commiſſioners, then ſuch clerks, officers or commiſſioners ſhall annex or affix unto ſuch will or codicil, or teſtamentary diſpoſition or inſtructions, or unto the cover, packet or parcel, which ſhall contain the ſame, a label or ſlip of parchment, upon which ſhall be written the name and deſcription of the

The manner of depoſiting wills, &c. fees to be paid.

teſtator

teſtator or teſtatrix, with ſome numerical figure or figures, and the name of the clerks, officers or commiſſioners, and the ſame ſhall be ſtampt with the ſtamp of the office, and that part of the label or ſlip of parchment, which ſhall contain the name of the clerks, officers or commiſſioners, and the numerical figure or figures, ſhall be cut off by an indented ſection, and delivered to the teſtator or teſtatrix, which being produced to the clerks, officers or commiſſioners of the ſaid reference office, or to their deputy or deputies, ſhall be to him or her a certificated authority to demand the delivery of the will, codicil, teſtamentary diſpoſition or inſtructions, or the packet or parcel, to which the ſame ſhall belong; and an entry ſhall be immediately forthwith made in the books, which the clerks, officers or commiſſioners for the time being, are hereby required to keep for that purpoſe in alphabetical and chronological order, of the day, on which the ſame was left or depoſited, and of the name and deſcription of the teſtator or teſtatrix, and of the numerical figure or figures expreſſed upon the label or ſlip of parchment as aforeſaid; and every ſuch entry ſhall be ſigned by the teſtator or teſtatrix, or his or her attorney or attornies for that particular purpoſe eſpecially authorized and deputed.

Manner of delivery of the wills, &c. to teſtator or teſtatrix.

And it is further declared and enacted by the authority aforeſaid, That whenever any perſon or perſons ſhall produce to the ſaid clerks, officers or commiſſioners, or their deputy or deputies, any ſuch label or ſlip of parchment ſo indented, ſtamped and ſigned as aforeſaid, every ſuch will, codicil, teſtamentary diſpoſition or inſtructions, or the packet or parcel, to which the ſame ſhall have been annexed

annexed or affixed, or ſhall belong, ſhall be delivered to the perſon or perſons producing ſuch label or ſlip of parchment as aforeſaid; and the entry thereof made in ſuch book or books as aforeſaid, ſhall be croſſed or marked, and the teſtator or teſtatrix ſo receiving back his or her will or codicil, teſtamentary diſpoſition or inſtructions, ſhall ſign in the margin of ſuch book or books oppoſite to the entry thereof, his or her name by way of acknowledging the receipt thereof; and every perſon to whom ſuch delivery ſhall be made, ſhall pay unto the ſaid clerks, officers or commiſſioners, the ſum of one ſhilling.

One ſhilling to be paid upon delivery of each will.

Provided always, and it is further declared and enacted by the authority aforeſaid, That no will, codicil, teſtamentary diſpoſition, nor inſtructions ſo depoſited as aforeſaid, ſhall be delivered to any other perſon or perſons, than the teſtator or teſtatrix, unleſs a power of attorney from the teſtator or teſtatrix ſhall be produced, together with ſuch certificated authority as aforeſaid properly executed, and authorizing the perſon or perſons producing ſuch certificated authority, label, or ſlip of parchment ſo indented, ſtampt, and ſigned as aforeſaid, to demand the delivery of the will or codicil, or packet or parcel, to which the ſame had been annexed or affixed, or did belong.

Manner of delivering wills to teſtator's attorney.

Provided always, and it is further declared and enacted by the authority aforeſaid, That every ſuch power of attorney, by virtue of which, any will, codicil, teſtamentary diſpoſition or inſtructions ſhall have been left or depoſited in ſuch office as aforeſaid, ſhall be depoſited, kept and delivered out, together with

The powers of attorney to be depoſited and delivered out with the wills.

with the will or codicil, packet or parcel, to which the ſame ſhall refer or belong.

Proviſo for delivery of wills in caſe the label or ſlip of parchment be loſt, &c.

And it is further declared and enacted by the authority aforeſaid, That in caſe any ſuch label or ſlip of parchment ſo indented, ſtampt, and ſigned as aforeſaid, ſhall be loſt, miſlaid, deſtroyed, or fraudulently obtained or ſuppreſſed from the teſtator or teſtatrix, or from his or her lawful attorney or attornies, then upon an affidavit having been made before a proper magiſtrate or magiſtrates of all the circumſtances of the caſe, as it ſhall have happened, and ſuch affidavit being produced to the ſaid clerks, officers or commiſſioners, or their deputy or deputies, they ſhall, and are hereby required to deliver out the will, codicil, teſtamentary diſpoſition or inſtructions, and the cover, packet or parcel, to which ſuch label or ſlip of parchment ſo indented, ſtampt and ſigned as aforeſaid ſhall have belonged, in the ſame manner, as if it had been actually produced, and the perſon or perſons receiving the ſame, by virtue of and under ſuch affidavit, ſhall ſign his, her or their name or names in the margin of the ſaid book or books as aforeſaid, oppoſite to the reſpective entry ſo to be croſſed or marked as aforeſaid, and add thereto the words, *by affidavit*; and the production of ſuch affidavit properly ſworn to and ſigned, ſhall be, and is hereby declared to be a full and ſufficient authority, warrant and indemnity to the clerks, officers or commiſſioners for delivering in conſequence thereof, ſuch will, codicil, packet or parcel as aforeſaid, againſt all perſons whomſoever.

Manner of delivering out wills after the death of teſtator.

Provided always, and it is further declared and enacted by the authority aforeſaid, That after the death of any perſon, who ſhall have ſo ſo depoſited his or her will, codicil, teſtamentary diſpoſition or inſtructions as aforeſaid, no ſuch will, codicil, teſtamentary diſpoſition nor inſtructions ſhall be delivered unto any perſon or perſons bringing ſuch label or ſlip of parchment ſo indented, ſtamped, and ſigned as aforeſaid, until a certificate of the burial of ſuch perſon ſo having died, ſhall have been produced, ſigned by the miniſter or prieſt of the pariſh or place where he ſhall have been buried; or in caſe of accidental death or no burial, until an affidavit of the death ſworn before a proper magiſtrate or magiſtrates of the place or country, where ſuch perſon ſhall have ſo died without having been buried, ſhall have been produced; and upon the production of any ſuch certificate or affidavit, the clerks, officers or commiſſioners, and their deputy or deputies, are hereby required to open ſuch will, codicil, teſtamentary diſpoſition or inſtructions as aforeſaid, in the preſence of the perſon or perſons producing ſuch label or ſlip of parchment ſo indented, ſtamped, and ſigned as aforeſaid, together with ſuch certificate or affidavit; and in caſe it ſhall appear, that ſuch perſon or perſons is or are intitled under ſuch will or codicil, either as executor or executrix, or executors or otherwiſe, to the poſſeſſion of ſuch will, codicil, teſtamentary diſpoſition or inſtructions, in order to prove or inrol the ſame, then the ſame ſhall be delivered to ſuch perſon or perſons accordingly, upon payment of the ſum of 2s. 6d. unto the ſaid officers, clerks or commiſſioners.

Fee of 2s. 6d. to be paid by the perſon receiving the will.

Provided neverthelesſs, and it is further declared and enacted by the authority aforeſaid, That any perſon or perſons producing ſuch certificate or affidavit of the burial or death of any

To whom wills to be delivered, in caſe of no certificated authority found.

any perſon to the ſaid clerks, officers or commiſſioners, although no ſuch label or ſlip of parchment, indented, ſtampt and ſigned as aforeſaid ſhall have been found in the poſſeſſion of the perſon ſo deceaſed, ſhall be intitled, upon paying the ſum of one ſhilling to the ſaid clerks, officers or commiſſioners, to ſearch all the books, in which any ſuch entries have been made as aforeſaid; and in caſe any ſuch will, codicil, teſtamentary diſpoſition or inſtructions ſhall be found to have been there left and depoſited by the perſon ſo deceaſed, the ſame ſhall immediately be opened and delivered upon payment of the additional ſum of 1s. 6d. to the ſaid clerks, officers or commiſſioners in manner aforeſaid.

And for what fees.

To whom wills to be delivered, when no executor.

Provided nevertheleſs, and it is further declared and enacted by the authority aforeſaid, That in caſe the perſon or perſons ſo producing ſuch label or ſlip of parchment, and ſuch certificate or affidavit as aforeſaid, ſhall not appear to be intitled to the poſſeſſion of ſuch will, codicil, teſtamentary diſpoſition or inſtructions, then the clerks, officers or commiſſioners, ſhall immediately give notice in writing to the executor or executrix, or executors in ſuch will or codicil named; or in caſe of none ſuch, to the perſon or perſons who ſhall appear to be intitled to the greateſt beneficial intereſt under the ſame, and ſhall deliver the ſame to ſuch perſon or perſons ſo reſpectively intitled as aforeſaid, or to his, her or their attorney or attornies for that purpoſe to be eſpecially appointed in manner aforeſaid, upon payment of two ſhillings and ſixpence to the clerks, officers or commiſſioners, in order that the ſame may be forthwith proved or inrolled as the law may require.

Upon Payment of [illegible]d.

Provided

Provided always, and it is further declared and enacted by the authority aforesaid, That whenever after the death of any such testator or testatrix, any such will or codicil, testamentary disposition or instructions, shall be delivered out of such office or repository, the person or persons, to whom the same shall be delivered, shall write his, her or their name or names in the margin of such book, opposite to the entry thereof as aforesaid, with such addition, as intitles him, her or them to the possession of such will, codicil, testamentary disposition or instructions.

Entries to be made in the books of the delivery, and to whom.

Provided nevertheless, and it is further declared and enacted by the authority aforesaid, That all such wills, codicils, testamentary dispositions or instructions, shall, before they are so deposited and entered as aforesaid, be covered with paper or parchment, and sealed by the person or persons depositing the same.

Wills to be sealed up when deposited.

And it is further declared and enacted by the authority aforesaid, That the said clerks, officers or commissioners appointed as aforesaid, and all deputies, whom they may employ in the execution of the said charge, office or commission, shall, before he or they shall respectively act therein, take and subscribe an oath before any one of the Judges of his Majesty's courts of record at Westminster, who are hereby authorized and impowered to administer the same in the form following, that is to say:

The oath to be taken not to open wills, till the act requires it.

"I A. B. do solemnly swear, that I will
"not open, nor permit nor procure to
"be opened, any packet or parcel, con-
"taining, or supposed to contain, any
"will, codicil, testamentary disposition
"or instructions, deposited or to be de-

N "posited

" posited in the reference office, by vir-
" tue of or under an act of parliament
" made and passed in the twenty-ninth
" year of the reign of his present Majesty,
" intituled, " *An act for requiring the*
" *inrolment of all deeds, wills and codi-*
" *cils relating to, touching or affecting*
" *any freehold and leasehold lands, te-*
" *nements or hereditaments within the*
" *kingdom of England and dominion of*
" *Wales, and for other purposes therein*
" *mentioned,*" whilst I shall continue to
" act as clerk, officer or commissioner
" thereof, (or as deputy to such clerk,
" officer or commissioner) but only in
" such cases in which the said act directs
" the same to be opened.

" So help me God."

Counterfeiting the names and handwritings of the clerks, felony.

And it is hereby further declared and enacted by the authority aforesaid, That if any person or persons shall forge or counterfeit the name or handwriting of any such officer, commissioner or clerk, or his deputy or deputies, or the stamp or seal of the said office, which shall have been made on such label or slip of parchment in manner aforesaid, according to the requisitions of and by virtue of this act, in order to procure the delivery or possession of any such will or codicil, testamentary disposition or instructions so deposited in the said office or repository as aforesaid, then every such person or persons so offending, being thereof lawfully convicted, shall be adjudged a felon or felons, and shall suffer death as in cases of felony without benefit of clergy.

*Obser-*

## *Obſervations upon the Draught of the Bill.*

I Beg leave generally to premiſe, that as my primary view in this publication, was to ſupply my readers with ſufficient matter, to enable them to form a ſatisfactory judgment upon the ſubject; ſo muſt I entreat them to conſider the draught of the bill as framed purpoſely for the ſuggeſtion of amendments by thoſe, who will take it under their conſideration; for *facile eſt inventis addere.* The leading principles of the bill, and the moſt material proviſions in it, are the immediate conſequences of the doctrine, which I have attempted to eſtabliſh. I cannot therefore be called upon to repeat, what may already appear to ſome to have been too diffuſely treated; though in didactic explanations and arguments upon profeſſional matters, written for nonprofeſſional readers, I conceive it to be the duty of the writer to omit nothing, which can tend to throw light upon the ſubject.

Although it be not very uſual, I hope it will be thought very proper, in altering and amending a law, to repeal all acts, which affect the law requiring ſuch alteration and amendment. There will then ariſe a general aſſurance and ſecurity, that nothing can affect the law in queſtion, which does not appear upon the face of that act, which undertakes openly to improve and aſcertain it.

It is to be obſerved, that the bill extends the inrolment to deeds and wills affecting all lands, (except copyhold and cuſtomary lands); for as they are always paſſed or affected with notoriety in the manor court, which generally is attended with ſome benefit or advantage to the lord of the manor, it will not be found juſt nor reaſonable to infringe the private rights of individuals by ſuper-inducing a public neceſſity over the private requi-ſition, from which the benefit aroſe to the indivi-dual. But there cannot be a ſhadow of pretence, why the inrolment ſhould not affect *leaſehold*, as well as *freehold* lands; for there certainly may be more opening to fraudulent and clandeſtine pre-conveyances and deceit, in the paſſing, altering and changing of leaſehold, than of freehold eſtates, becauſe at preſent leſs notoriety attends the former than the latter.

The payments directed to be made to the per-ſons ſigning the warrants, *fiats*, or directions for in-rolment, are regulated according to the preſent uſages; and in the ſame proportion all the other payments throughout the bill are framed.

The proviſions made for ſecuring the proper number of ſtamps to each deed and will inrolled, is a matter which affects the finance, more than the regulation of the law of the country. There can-not be a doubt, but that the legiſlature in paſſing the 20th of his preſent Majeſty meant, that there ſhould be a ſtamp for each ſkin of fifteen common law ſheets; and it is well known by experience and practice, that ſeveral of the moſt reputable perſons of the profeſſion, make it a general practice to in-ſert a greater number of words in the ſkin under one ſtamp, than evidently the act of parliament in-tended ſhould be allowed or permitted. This act, which undertakes to regulate and aſcertain the matter, does not poſitively enact, that ſuch a quan-tity of words ſhall be confined to one ſtamp; but that, if any perſon having charged his client for in-groſſing more, than fifteen common law folios un-der one ſtamp, ſhall be open to an information, and

liable

liable to a penalty of twenty pounds. Now, as most deeds at present are secret conveyances, and not exposed to public inspection, this is a matter, which seldom extends beyond the knowledge and privacy of the sollicitor and client; but how impossible is it, that the former should lodge an information to profit of his own inattention to or nonobservance of the law? And how improbable, that the latter should inform against his own sollicitor, for having saved him a considerable expence by evading the duty upon stamps? The only secure method of compelling persons to use a proper number of stamps to a given number of words, is by invalidating the deed, if it be not properly stamped: this would give occasion to much altercation and suspicion amongst individuals, if it were made to depend upon their scrutiny and judgment; therefore the clerks of the inrolment office, are made the judges of the fact, and their judgment is rendered liable to very heavy penalties, upon information within a reasonable limitation of time. The vigilance therefore of the clerks will prevent the revenue from being injured, and the actual inrolment of deeds, wills and codicils, will secure individuals from any risk or danger of their becoming invalid, from a want of the proper number of stamps.

As the credibility and responsibility of the officers, clerks or commissioners of the different courts or offices, are objects which ought to be well attended to, and as all popular elections are constantly attended with dissention, dissipation, and many other disadvantages and inconveniencies, I have ventured to suggest a new mode of election, upon this principle, that a person chosen by the majority of the representatives of the country, will be more impartially and quietly elected, than in any other manner: for

for it is to be presumed, that party influence, family and pecuniary considerations, or other private views of partiality, will not operate so forcibly upon the members of parliament, as they may be supposed to do upon other individuals, more closely connected with the persons likely to be chosen.

It would be harsh and unjust to deprive the present Yorkshire registers of their appointments; and if reasonable for others, it would be absurd not to have this county adopt the general mode of election in future.

If, however, this mode of election be not relished, there is nothing more easy, than to substitute that in its lieu, which now prevails in the county of York.

As to Middlesex, as the officers and clerks are now in the nomination of the heads of the four courts of records, it would be very unjust and unwarrantable to deprive such respectable characters, as fill these employs, of that patronage, which has usually been annexed to their offices; and as in future more business will certainly come through these offices by the inrolment, than by the registry of deeds and wills, the patronage will be proportionably greater, than it has heretofore been.

As London is the center of most money transactions negociated in this nation, it is needless to state a reason, why a reference office should be fixed there, rather than in any other place; and the propriety of its existence will fully appear, from the many occasions, which occur in London of searching for the inrolment of deeds and wills inrolled in distant counties; and much delay, doubt, and expence will be avoided, by the order and regularity of such reference books: there is no public office or conservatory, which has not within itself such books of reference; the utility and advantage of which,

which, are fully known and felt by all perſons, who have occaſion to make ſearches amongſt public archives and records. I ſhall then ſay no more upon the ſubject, than that, if there be county inrolment offices, or courts eſtabliſhed, there ſhould alſo be national books of reference to them, in order, as much as poſſible, to concenter into one point the whole knowledge, that is intended and required to be conveyed to the public, by recording all deeds and wills affecting lands.

I know many inſtances, in which wills have been ſuppreſſed after the deaths of the teſtators, by the perſons, into whoſe poſſeſſion they fell; but I need not enter into a detail of the very ſerious conſequences, which may thereby happen to the perſons intereſted under ſuch wills. Many caſes have happened, and poſſibly many more may happen, in which wills have been, and may be altered, miſlaid and deſtroyed, wilfully and by accident. And therefore, as I have endeavoured to ſuggeſt a plan of general practical utility, reſpecting deeds and deviſes, I have conſidered it as an extenſion of that plan, to provide a ſafe conſervatory, where all perſons expoſed to travel, either by ſea or land, having no fixt reſidence, or no ſecure repoſitory within that reſidence, or diffiding in thoſe, who either during their lives, or after their deaths, may have acceſs to their private papers, may depoſit their wills with ſafety, where they will be preſerved in ſecrecy, and from whence they will be delivered out to ſuch perſons only, who will be intitled to receive them. As there is no eſtabliſhment of the nature elſewhere in the kingdom, I have from my own ideas, endeavoured to chalk out a plan of ſuch order, regularity, and conveniency in it, as I think will beſt anſwer the intended purpoſes.

Con-

Convinced as I am, and long have been, that a general Inrolment Aćt will be of very eſſential benefit to the nation, I claim that indulgence from my readers, which a generous public will ever allow to every ſerious attempt to ſerve one's country; to do which will ever be the firſt ambition of my life.

*F I N I S.*

www.ingramcontent.com/pod-product-compliance
Lightning Source LLC
Chambersburg PA
CBHW030556040726
47497CB00008B/2745

* 9 7 8 3 3 3 7 2 0 7 8 8 5 *